OF THE BLOOD

Crowns Volume III

James B Lynch

ISBN-13: 978-0-9915221-3-2
ISBN-10: 1477123456

Cover design by: James B Lynch
Library of Congress Control Number: 2018675309
Printed in the United States of America

BOOK 1: NINJAS AND DRAGONS

CHAPTER 1

The Kaian Star Empire was vast. So expansive was it that it would be impossible for anyone to traverse its breadth in a single lifetime without the use of fast-than-light fold drive technology. Were one of its kings or queens from generations past brought forward in time, they'd have recognized little but its core worlds.

At the edge of Kaian space, a pair of modest shuttles glided through the inky darkness. The light metals and soft curves of their hulls were illuminated only by dull running lights that dotted their frames.

Unassuming in appearance and not proud in stature, the crimson markings along their skins identified them as fully commissioned vessels representing the seat of the empire.

Soldiers in service of the crown huddled in each gleaming, bench-lined cargo hold. Some checked their gear; others conversed in small groups. All were adorned in the green-piped uniforms of the general infantry.

Sat nearest to the rear hatch in the starboard vessel was a rough man called Thque. The stripes on his shoulders denoted his leadership of these troops; the lines on his face only served to reinforce that notion.

Sitting furthest from the exit was, in many ways, Thque's opposite. The young, fresh-faced man – barely that, even – was motionless, like he was afraid any movement would attract attention he did not want. The patch across the breast of his jacket identified him as Cabe.

"Hey, new guy."

The only indication of a reaction from Cabe to Thque's granite voice was a slight widening of the eyes. He otherwise remained frozen in his chosen seat.

Thque motioned for Cabe to join him at the rear of the compartment. Hesitantly, he unrooted himself and made his way towards the far end of the cabin. Upon the boy's arrival, Thque pointed to an empty seat across the crowded aisle.

Cabe sat.

"This's your first job." Thque's words attacked Cabe's eardrums. "Lemme guess, you just wanted to hang at the back of the crowd, observe, not get in the way."

Cabe shrugged.

"Bit of advice: don't. Stick by the guys who know what they're doing. And nobody here knows what they're doing more than me." Thque nodded to the man sat to his left, a visage nearly as worn and frazzled as his own. "If I'm not around, Fra's the next best guy. You have any questions, ask 'em. But don't test that adage about the only dumb question being the one you don't ask. There are plenty of dumb questions."

Cabe nodded.

Thque's eyes narrowed. "You don't talk much, do you?"

Cabe shrugged again. "My mama always taught me that if you don't have anything to say it's better to keep your mouth shut."

"Your mama sounds like a smart gal."

"Nah, she's dumber than a bag of bricks," Cabe said. "She just didn't want to have to hear from us."

The two elder men shared a laugh with their young compatriot.

"You gonna be alright down there?" Thque asked once the merriment had subsided.

"I'm just worried," Cabe said.

"About what? Dragons?"

"Yeah."

"Don't be," Thque said assuredly. "Dragons are huge. You can see 'em coming a mile away. There're all sorts of other things that can sneak up on you. Those are the little buggers you have to watch out for."

"What kinds of things?"

"Oh, insects, mostly."

Cabe chuckled. "Insects?"

Thque held up his snarled hand.

"Yeah, no bigger than my thumbnail."

"It's a nature preserve," Cabe said. "They can't be spreading diseases, can they?"

Thque leaned back, letting the bones of his spine unfurl into the shape of the seat.

"No, nothing like that," he said breathily.

"So they're poisonous then?"

"No, no."

Cabe nodded, a weak movement of his neck that barely bobbed his head.

"Okay, good."

"Venomous," Thque said. "Poisonous means you get sick when you eat them. Venomous is when you get sick from them chomping you. Some of these buggers'll put gunk in your body enough to melt your muscles and explode your heart."

"That doesn't really calm my nerves."

"Not trying to. I'm trying to keep your dumb ass alive."

Thque folded his arms and dropped his hat over the cloudy pools of his eyes, settling in for the remainder of the trip.

CHAPTER 2

The ships found land in a jungle clearing. Dense foliage spilled out in every direction for as far as the eye could see, save for the singular bald spot where the silver craft made their nest.

The rear of the ships split along a line parallel to the ground, roughly halfway up the slanted section of hull. Each half moved in tandem, one rising over the top of the vessel while the other forged itself into a ramp for the occupants.

Thque was the first out, enthusiastically bounding down the sloped metal walkway. Behind him, Cabe hesitated, stopping progress for the rest of the company.

Without the need to turn back, Thque could tell he was alone on the patch of the planet's surface. He glanced over his shoulder to discern the cause.

"You alright, kid?"

"Yeah." Gingerly, Cabe made his way down the ramp. "I just wasn't expecting the smell."

"Yeah, planet full of wild animals. Who'd have guessed it'd smell like piss and flop?"

Rather than taking the incline down, Fra climbed off to one side and hopped the full way, past the swarm of bodies pushing to be free of the cramped confines of the cargo hold. It was no more than a couple of meters and his calloused body seemed no worse for wear.

"What're you thinking, boss?" he asked as he approached

Thque.

"What makes you think I'm thinking anything?"

"'Cause you're the big brains of the operation."

Thque smirked. "The warden should've been out here to meet us."

"Are we early?" Cabe asked.

"No," Thque said, "we're right on time."

"If we'd been late he might've gotten tired of waiting and gone back inside," Fra reasoned.

Thque pulled a small metal timepiece from his pants pocket and flipped it open. The blue glow from within reflected across his leathery skin.

"But we're not late. We said we'd be here at nineteen hundred, it's nineteen hundred on the dot right now."

"So, what're you thinking?" Fra repeated.

"I'm thinking we find the warden." Thque raised his hand over his head and motioned to the troops. "Blue team, with us. Black team, stay back and get things prepped for the transfer."

One of the men from the other ship gave a half-hearted salute. He and his compatriots went to work in the rear hangar of their ship.

Thque adjusted the shoulder strap on his weapon and headed off into the jungle. The team from his ship fell in behind him, moving close to single-file through the thick undergrowth.

Relatively speaking, it did not take long for them to reach the planet's welcome center: a gray, flat building, much broader than it was tall, pecked into the middle of the vegetation.

And still the whole of the way there they'd not encountered any signs of intelligent life.

"We're practically in his house now," said Fra. "We should've heard something."

Thque held his rifle at the ready. "Yup."

They approached the building from the front. It was in an

opened state; the front door was wide enough to accommodate several people side-by-side.

The group entered cautiously, firearms held steady.

In the darkness, something small chirped and scurried out the rear of the building.

When fully closed down, the welcome center was essentially a small fortress, primarily used for monitoring the wildlife on the planet. A station set off to the right had a chair sat before a bank of screens; to the left was a simple bed and stacks of personal effects.

The first thing they noticed was the monitoring station. In the dull light provided by the screens, and backlit by the light from the building's rear, the chair could be seen to be askew, pushed away from the workspace and spun about. Work tablets lay scattered about the desktop, their screens still illuminated.

Not just on the desk, but on the concrete floor around it.

Thque sniffed at the air.

"You smell that?"

"I'm still smelling outside," Cabe said.

"Something's burning." He motioned to Fra, who took several of the troops and fanned out towards the makeshift living space.

Thque himself headed for the desk, moving past the chair and kneeling beside the machinery beneath the console.

He sniffed at the air again, getting down on his hands and knees to make his way towards an access panel on the machine.

"Well. Shit."

"What is it?" Cabe moved in closer, still gripping his weapon.

Thque raised back up to one knee.

"Something burning inside the console. That can't be good."

"Could it be it overheated?" Cabe asked.

"Could be. This planet's hotter than a mola bear's balls. Warden out here on his own most of the time, if it couldn't be repaired..."

Fra wandered over and poked at one of the active screens. "That ain't the worst of it," he said.

Thque rose to his feet and patted his hands. "Why's that?"

Fra turned the monitor towards his commanding officer. "Enclosure's failed."

"Crap."

Cabe's gaze darted back and forth between the two men. "What does that mean?"

"It means nothing's keeping the animals separated except for some fence posts and wires," said Thque.

"Okay, but... so what?" the younger man asked. "It's not like they're gonna be flying off-world on their own power."

"Without enclosure, the bigger predators are going to encounter one another eventually," Thque said. "Animals might start migrating out of their habitat zones. Whole species of animals will fight, eat, or otherwise kill themselves to extinction."

"Half the creatures on this planet don't exist anywhere else anymore," Fra added. "They die here, they're gone for good."

"Technically, some of them have genetic samples in storage back on Kaia and could be cloned back into existence," Thque said, "but the damage to the environment here would be catastrophic."

Fra shrugged. "Ain't much point in cloning a thing to life if you've got nowhere to house it after."

Thque gave a nod.

"Exactly. Plus cloning a species back isn't the same as an unbroken lineage. It feels... unnatural. And wrong."

Cabe put his hands up, letting his rifle swing freely to his side.

"Okay, I get it, I get it. So, what do we do to reestablish enclosure?"

"We don't," Thque said. "We find that damn warden and see what he needs to get it done."

Fra let out a slow breath.

"What if what he needs is to place a call back to Kaia for

reinforcements?"

"We are the reinforcements," Thque said. "Ain't no help coming from the royals, especially not this week. We've got enough manpower to put every beasty on this world back where it goes if we need to, but we don't reactivate enclosure until we can be reasonably certain they're there."

CHAPTER 3

Thque and Fra stayed near the console, poking around its inner workings, while most of the rest of the troops prepared to depart.

Fra sat upright and wiped his brow.

"Hey, look at this."

"What is it?" Thque asked, nudging closer.

Fra gestured through the open port.

"The enclosure system. It didn't fail, or just get shut off. It's been totally sabotaged."

"Let me in there." Thque forced his way past his friend, nearly crawling inside the port. "Goddamn. Like someone ripped all the pieces out then torched the whole thing."

"Don't we got a repair crew with us?" Cabe asked. He was the only one of the troops not prepping their gear for departure.

"We got a couple of guys with some tools," Fra said.

"And parts," said Thque. "It can't hurt for them to have a look at it."

It wasn't too long before the group made it back to their ships.

Fra was the first to break away from the platoon, approaching a small gathering of troops from the other vessel. They spoke briefly before heading back out into the jungle.

Thque relaxed his grip on his weapon as he climbed atop a stack of crates and looked out at his people.

"Okay, we got a bad news/bad news situation here. Which you want first?" The troops all stared at him. "Okay, bad news first. As you may have noticed, we returned without the one dragon we were here to pick up for delivery. The conservation warden is currently MIA and the welcome center is trashed. Our dragon doesn't seem to have been prepped for us."

The group grunted and groaned.

"Now the bad news. Enclosure has failed; near as we can tell, planet-wide. Not only is our dragon not here, we don't know where it is, either by tracking or by checking its habitat, because its habitat zone has now expanded to the size of the whole goddamn planet. And reestablishing enclosure right now, even if we could, would just hold everything where it is now, which is not where it's supposed to be, and we have to assume there's not necessarily a lot of overlap in those two things."

"What's the mean for us?" someone in the sweaty group asked.

"It means our mission parameters have changed. We're not here just picking up one dragon anymore, we're here fixing the whole of the ecosphere."

More groans.

"We've got the equipment and the numbers to do it. It's up to all y'all to prove to me we've got the quality of people to get it done." The grumbling came again, a bit quieter this time. "Yeah. Get out the speeders. Prep the ships. I want ship two in the air before I'm done giving this speech. Ship one needs to be converted for transport. We're gonna be tranqing these holy beasts and dropping them back where they should go. You've got planetary maps in your databanks. Let's make this fast. We can't have any of these things waking the hell back up before enclosure's reactivated, and I don't want to have to waste any time retracing our steps to drug any of 'em back up once they're where they ought to be."

"What about the ones in the water?"

"If they're in the water and they ought to be, leave 'em there. If they're there and they're not supposed to be, well, they're probably dead already."

The assembled crew members shrugged and mumbled their agreement.

"The welcome center is base camp," Thque said. "Me, Fra, and a few of the others will hang behind and see if we can't suss out what happened to the warden."

Thque hopped down from his makeshift stage and motioned for several members of his group, Cabe included, to follow him back into the brush. The rest of the crew got to work on the ships.

CHAPTER 4

Cabe came across Thque kneeling in the foliage near to the welcome center.

"Hey," said Cabe.

Thque did not look back at him.

"What can I do for you?"

"I came to see if I could be of help."

"No offense, kid, but the best way for you to help right now is to stay away from me."

"Oh." Cabe watched Thque peer intently at the ground. "What're you doing?"

"Trying to get a trail. I used to be a tracker way back in my early days of service. I should be able to pick up some sign of where the warden's been."

"And can you?"

Thque shook his head.

"Nothing fresh."

"Well, we don't know for sure how long he's been missing," Cabe offered.

"We were last in contact with him a few days back. I'm not finding anything newer'n that."

"Well then."

"Yeah." Thque's knees creaked as he stood, loud enough to warn off any nearby animals. If he was worried about the effect Cabe's conversing would have on the natural order of the nearby wildlife, his own aging body had just done far worse. "I'm not giving up, though."

"That's admirable, I guess."

"Not looking for your approval."

The color drained from Cabe's face.

Before either man could breech the awkwardness between them, they heard a sharp, popping ring from deeper in the jungle.

Then another, and more and more following.

Gunfire. And lots of it.

"What in the holy hell?" Thque took off running.

Even with his younger, fresher extremities, it took Cabe all he had to keep up as Thque tore his way through the vegetation.

They came upon a collection of their fellow troops on the far side of the welcome center. The soldiers stood in a circular formation. All around them was a ring of spent bullet casings. Some still let off short bursts into the trees.

Thque's arms flailed into their line of sight as he approached.

"What in the hell is going on?"

"Something in the trees, boss," one of the soldiers replied.

"What?"

"What do you mean..."

"I mean what was in the trees?" Thque asked.

"We don't know."

"You don't know." Thque took a solid breath. "You're on a planet full of endangered animals and you just start shooting at shit without even knowing what you're aiming at?"

"Well we weren't actually sure."

"Sure of what?"

"What we were aiming at," the soldier said. "We saw movement, but it was hard to pin down just where it was. So, we took a circular pattern and..."

"Oh, I see. You didn't just shoot indiscriminately into the

jungle. You shot up the whole damn jungle. Does that seem better to you?"

"Not when you put it that way."

"Tell me any way that it could be put where it sounds better," Thque said.

"Well..."

Thque glared at him.

"I mean..." the man stammered.

Thque's eyes bulged out.

"I'm telling you," the soldier said, "there was something in those trees."

The optical orbs that had just popped from their sockets now rolled back beneath the upper lid.

Another soldier piped up.

"He's telling the truth, boss. Whatever it was, it took out Dell and Mios."

Thque squinted at them.

"Took them out meaning...?"

Thque and several of the others stood over Dell's body, missing an arm and part of the shoulder and chest area on the left side.

Having just arrived, Thque squatted down beside what was left of him.

"I told you," one of the men said.

"Well, we're all thinking it, I suppose," said Thque.

"Thinking of what?"

"Whatever did this to 'em, it left the bodies here. Warden's missing, could be he's already been et by some creature or another. An animal wouldn't normally leave a fresh kill behind like this, though." Thque reached down and turned the body to get a better look. "This is weird. No bullet, no shrapnel. You find any casings?"

"We tried fanning out but couldn't find nothing but our

own rounds."

"What are you thinking, boss?" asked Fra.

Thque stood up.

"Well, something blew his whole arm clean off."

"That ain't what I'd call clean," said Cabe.

"Fair enough. So either we got some kind of predator after us, or it was a someone that took out the warden, and they're still around."

"You think someone stuck around after that?" Fra asked.

"Not convinced it was a someone," said Thque. "There's more than one type of thing living on this world that could take a man apart."

"Without being seen?" Fra asked.

"Some of the guys did see something," said Thque.

"Something that disappeared into the trees without a trace," said Fra.

"And there's more than one thing on this world that can camouflage itself," said Thque. "The enclosure system's down, what about the rest of it?"

"Rest of the control room looked like it was pretty much intact," said Fra.

"Let's go see about it," said Thque. "Something's hunting us. And if it wasn't a person did this, then that means they're hunting for sport, not food. I want to know what."

CHAPTER 5

Fra approached Thque as he sat at the warden's desk, focused on the screens directly ahead of him.

"Any luck?" Fra asked.

"Based on what we know?" asked Thque. "Nah. Narrowed it down a little bit."

Fra hunched forward and peered over Thque's shoulder.

"Could be a eeltor," Fra said.

"We're a little far from the water," said Thque. "But maybe, if it was desperate. I'm leaning more towards a serpanthor. They're stealthy enough, and the females do project acid."

"That didn't look like an acid burn on them bodies."

"I know."

"It seems we're ignoring the obvious."

"Which is?"

"We ain't alone here," said Fra.

"I keep thinking that. But if we ain't, where's their ship? How'd they even get on a cordoned-off preserve? We only got in 'cause of our royal credentials."

"Could be the warden lowered the defenses."

"That don't right make a ton of sense," said Thque. "He lets somebody onto the preserve then they torch the controls?"

"Could any animal do that to the control system?"

"I don't know. There's animals smart enough to tear out the controls maybe, and there's animals that spit fire, but not a lot of crossover 'tween the two."

"We came here to pick up a dragon," said Fra. "They're smart and make fire."

Thque looked up at him.

"They're also about twenty times too big to fit through the door at full size, and as far as we know there hasn't been a birth in years."

"Could be the warden did it himself for some reason?" Fra suggested.

"I keep trying to come through with a scenario where that makes sense. Warden doing maintenance and gets attacked? But that don't explain why everything inside was yanked rough the way it was."

"Or," said Fra, "someone got to him and ripped it apart after they did whatever they did to him."

"But to what end? A wild animal could be just doing what comes natural. If it was a person did this, I can't suss out the why."

"Could be they was poachers," Fra said.

"Really? Why'd poachers knock out enclosure? Why not just go out and get whatever animals they thought they'd want."

"Do we really need to know the why of it?" Fra asked.

"I guess we'd just need to know there is a 'why' to it in order to determine it was a person that did this and not an animal," said Thque.

They fell silent at the sound of hard soles against the concrete floor. It took the pair of them a moment to recognize the shape entering the dim facility as belonging to Cabe.

"Hey, boss, guys think they found something," he said.

Thque and Fra shared a look before heading out.

An hour later, Cabe, Thque, Fra, and about five others stalked their way through the jungle.

"You said we'd be able to see it coming a mile away," Cabe said.

They came to a rest where Cabe pointed to a still form laid out among the flora.

A dead dragon.

About 30 meters long from snout to tail with an even wider wingspan, it did not land in a clearing but crushed down the trees to make way. It hit the dirt belly-down, its thick hide unscathed by the branches and trunks beneath it. Its tail, making up nearly half the length of its body, curled off through the foliage, twisting just a bit to expose the lighter colored scales along its front. The wings, thick flesh stretched between lengths of bone, took on the shape of the landscape beneath them. At a glance, nothing on its body appeared to have been damaged when it came down.

"Don't get smart with me, kid," said Thque.

"This the one we came here to transport?" Fra asked.

"Hard to tell," said Thque. "The tagging system went down with enclosure. The one we came looking for was pregnant, though. This one doesn't seem to be."

"How'd it die?" asked Cabe.

Thque barely ran his eyes over the downed beast.

"No obvious markings on the body, unless they're on the underside. But I don't see any blood pooling or anything like that, either. We won't be able to say much else without an autopsy, which we are very much not in a position to perform."

"So we're looking for something that can take out a dragon without leaving a mark but blows limbs right off of men, is that it?" asked Fra.

"There're very few things in the universe that can take out a dragon at all, much less do it cleanly," said Thque.

"Then why are they endangered?" asked Cabe. Thque glared at him. "I'm just asking."

"Dragons have a tendency to overbreed in the wild," Thque said. "They deplete natural resources. The opposite problem happens in captivity. They almost never reproduce."

"Well I can't fault 'em there," said Fra. "I'd have a hard time breeding with a bunch of zoologists watching me, too."

"The one we came for was the first one giving birth in almost two decades," said Thque. "The queen is not gonna be happy about all this."

"The queen ain't never gonna be happy with a thing we do," said Fra.

"Well there is that. We should get back to camp, but..." Thque stopped short at the sound of squawking nearby. "Hold."

The entire group raised their weapons and sightlines towards the trees.

"That the sound you heard before you all started shooting up the jungle?" Thque asked.

One of the soldiers shook his head.

"Didn't hear a call."

They moved almost in unison, stepping towards the thick of the jungle.

"Down," Thque said flatly.

A swarm of flying creatures burst from the trees. Each one a meter long and twice as wide: segmented bodies and translucent wings.

The group dropped to the dirt where they stood.

Cabe raised his gun and stared down the sight. Before he could make any further movement, Thque pushed the barrel down.

"Wait," Thque said.

"Wait?" Cabe asked.

"Wait," Thque repeated. "Look at 'em."

The dense covering of creatures sped past and descended upon the dragon carcass.

"They're not after us, unless we go and rile 'em up."

"What the hell are those things?" Cabe asked.

"Scavengers. Bugs."

"Bugs?" asked Cabe.

"Yup."

"You told me the bugs on this planet were as big as a thumbnail."

"Some of 'em are."

"You think these are what took down the dragon?" asked Cabe.

"No way. These things showing up this late, picking at the body. If they'd been what took it down, they'd have been here feasting this whole time."

Thque raised his arm and signaled for the team to move out.

The seven of them rose up, dusted themselves off, and started back for the welcome center.

They got a ways into the jungle, away from the bugs and the dragon, before Thque really took stock of the team.

They stumbled to a halt behind their commander, who'd stopped mid stride.

"Wait a sec," Thque said. "Where the hell's... uh..."

"Juckz," said Fra.

"Yeah, her," said Thque. "We'd notice if the bugs got her."

The others looked around.

"Anybody seen her?" Thque asked. "Anybody seen where she went to?"

"Did she maybe wander off?" Cabe asked. "Have to take a leak or something?"

"You think she's that dumb?" Thque asked.

"I don't know her well enough to say," said Cabe.

"I do, and she might be," said Fra.

Thque grunted and gripped his weapon. "Well we're not waiting for her."

"You figuring she's dead?" asked Fra.

"I'm figuring, yeah. I'd stay and see if we could find where she went either way, but I'm not staying here. Get back to base camp, double-time." He looked around the trees. "And keep your eyes open. On the trees and each other. I don't want nobody else getting disappeared."

The group made their way through the thicket at a brisk clip, continually glancing around, up into the canopy.

At some point on their journey, either to or from the dragon's corpse, they must have unknowingly altered their course. Arriving at the river that ran between the two points, they found themselves stood before wider and deeper water than expected. Not willing to take any chances, they were forced to make their way to a narrow crossing.

As they did so, the water beside them suddenly bubbled. It was only a matter of seconds before a great form, serpentine in appearance, sprang forth from beneath the gentle ripples of the streaming water, rising high over the soldiers' heads.

The troopers had no time to react, being partially blinded as the murky liquid was flung from the beast's long, shiny back in all directions.

It lunged for the group with a maw full of curved fangs, snatching one of them up with a wet crunch that alerted his still-unsteady compatriots to his fate before he even had the chance to call out. Muscles within its mouth forced the screaming, thrashing soldier down its throat.

"Holy hell!" Cabe screamed.

"This one you can shoot at!" yelled Thque.

Their vision clearing, the remainder of the group lifted their weapons and opened fire.

A monstrous roar belted out as the animal reared back, the twitching limbs of its victim still visible through its teeth.

"I thought we were here as conservationists," Fra yelled to Thque as they blasted at the massive water snake.

"We are," Thque replied.

After several rounds of blasting from the remaining soldiers, the creature retreated back beneath the river, leaving a faint reddening of the water behind.

Cabe stomped out ahead of the group, his face frozen in a panicked shock.

"I am sick and tired of every goddamn thing on this planet trying to kill us!"

"Take it easy, kid," said Thque. "They're just animals. This's their way."

"I don't care if it's their way, I don't want their way killing me!"

"Best to just keep moving."

Uneasily clutching their weapons, the group continued on.

They returned to an empty welcome center. Even the light from the monitors had abandoned the place.

"Where the hell is everybody?" Fra asked.

"I didn't see anybody watching the perimeter either," said Cabe.

Thque went for the comms system.

"Team one, check in."

There was no response.

He held the microphone towards his face again.

"Team two, check in."

Still nothing.

"What're you thinking?" Fra asked him.

"Stop asking me what I'm thinking. I'm thinking the same damn thing all of you are. Something's been taking our people out. Either animals or a hostile force. We've lost contact with two well-armed transports and our people keep vanishing into thin air."

"What could down a transport though?" Cabe asked. "Without us seeing it, I mean. Without even giving them a chance to signal us."

Thque racked his brain.

"Stealth ships. Camazars."

Fra harrumphed.

"Stealth ships. Huh."

"I ain't gonna ask you what you're thinking," Thque said. "Out with it."

"Whatever took off Dell's arm like that, could've been a ship-based launcher."

"Would have to be a pretty weak one," Thque said. "And to not leave any burns in the trees?"

"What everybody was shooting at, seeing something in the trees, could've been jet-wash," said Fra.

"Something about that just isn't adding up. But we don't have any better theories just yet, so I'll keep it in mind."

"Is anything adding up?" Cabe asked.

Thque glared at him.

"What the hell did you just say to me?"

"I'm asking; nothing about this makes any sense. You can't suss out if it was an animal or people that did this. What kind of animal, if it was one. No two things about it are adding up. If you can't work it out, what are any of us going to do?"

"So what do you want to do?" Thque asked him.

"I don't even know. I'd say we cut our losses and run, but we can't even reach our ships."

"We came to the royal preserve to transport one of the queen's dragons. Something out there is killing us. If it's people, they're willing and able to take on royal armed forces. If it's animals, it's enough to kill us off and bring down a dragon." Thque looked up at the darkening sky. "We're losing daylight. We should set up for the night. New guy, you're on first watch."

"Me?"

"There a problem?"

"Yeah," said Cabe. "I don't wanna die. Our people have been getting picked off left and right. Putting one guy on watch…"

"We don't have enough bodies left for much more'n that," said Thque. "Everybody else get some shuteye. We'll relieve you in a few hours."

CHAPTER 6

Most of the team was forced to sleep in chairs or on the floor, as Thque took the only bed available. It belonged to the missing warden, and in other circumstances, claiming it may have come across as macabre.

Cabe passed his relief on the way in.

"Back already?" Thque asked.

"Shouldn't you be asleep?"

"Hard to with someone marching around the whole of the building."

"S'what happens when you put one guy on watch."

A strange noise shot through the place: undefinable to their ears. They, as well as all the others in the place, bolted upright.

"Grab your gear." Thque started pulling on his boots while the others made for their guns. Cabe, already dressed and armed from his watch, ran for the front door. "Hold on, kid! Don't go out there alone."

Cabe stopped. "Uh, I'm getting very mixed messages here."

It was only a matter of moments before the others had hurriedly dressed and geared up.

The remaining five soldiers exited the center and looked around. In the best of circumstances, the heavy leaf coverage lowered visibility to a crippling degree. Having to search by what little moonlight filtered through didn't make the job any easier.

"Anybody see Andler?" Thque asked.

"Not a trace," said Fra.

An unfamiliar screeching echoed out from the jungle.

"Was that a dragon?" Fra asked.

"Not a full-grown one," said Thque.

"What would that mean?" Fra asked. "The mare birthed early?"

"Not sure a newborn could make all this happen," said Thque.

"Dragons are smart though," said Cabe.

"Yeah." Thque gave a single nod. "Smart enough to coordinate an attack, maybe. But to stay hidden like this?"

"Well, like the kid said earlier, no two pieces of this are fitting together," said Fra.

"I got a feeling we're gonna be finding out the answer to all of this sooner rather than later." Thque took hold of his rifle and sprayed wildly into the forest. "Come out! Come out and face us! Damn cowards!"

He fired again.

The jungle fell eerily quiet after he'd released the trigger.

"This is bull," he said through gritted teeth. "Sitting out there, picking us off like animals. I'm the hunter here! Me!"

He lifted his rifle again, this time raising the sight to his eye. The last thing he saw through it was an arrow coming straight towards him, punching through the scope.

He only just managed to avoid being impaled.

Having witnessed the incident up close, Fra let out with a, "Holy shit!"

The others started firing into the woods.

Another arrow came. This one stuck into the ground and exploded, sending the remaining troops scattering.

Thque picked a knife from his boot and squeezed the handle in his palm.

"Whoever's out there, you should know we're here with the full authority of the crown. Whatever you do to us, the queen'll return to you tenfold."

Laughter boomed back at him. With the echoing of the

environment, it was impossible to determine the source, if it had a singular origin.

"Well that's unsettling," said Cabe.

"They're out there. Laughing at us," said Thque. "Really wish I'd know who it was before we die. How many of 'em it took to take all of us…"

Another arrow flew in, catching him in the shoulder. He spun around as his body flopped to the dirt.

"Holy hell!" Cabe belted out.

The remaining troops fired into the trees again.

From out of the brush a few meters away, a shadowing figure charged the men. The soldiers didn't even have time to adjust their aim before it was upon them, slamming one to the ground and tossing another into the air.

Thque somehow managed to drag himself shakily to his feet, still clutching the small knife.

"One?" he balked. "It was just one of you?!"

He lunged for the shape, the blade held out straight in front of him. It was easily smacked away.

Only then did he get a clear look at his opponent.

"Oh. Oh, goddammit…"

He dropped to the ground.

Cabe, lying a short distance away, raised his weapon.

The dark stranger quickly had a bow out and an arrow nocked.

The arrow crackled with a winding white energy that ran up and down its shaft.

"Oh, God…" Cabe recoiled, covering his head with his arms.

The dark figure relaxed her bowing arm.

"You pissed yourself," she said.

Cabe looked up again. The figure before him was dark even in spite of the lack of illumination in the region. Her body was covered in metal plating, a pleasing mixture of cool and warm hues. Across the front of her helmet was a spiked faceplate with at least five distinct points.

Across her back was a simple canvas pack that held a heavy reptilian creature. Wings and head poked out and over her shoulder. The thing's head featured a pronounced snout; a short, boney fin ran directly between oversized eyes that glistened in the sparse moonlight.

Even a simple man like Cabe was able to recognize Valentina, Queen of the Kaian Empire, and a baby dragon.

"What?" he managed to choke out.

"You pissed yourself," she said. "Your trousers are soaked in urine. Your own, I'm assuming."

"Oh, this is embarrassing."

"You think it's bad? Try having enhanced senses when some poacher empties his bladder at your feet."

He was very near to tears.

"I'm sorry. This was my first job. I just needed the money. Please don't kill me."

"I've already decided I'm not. Don't give me a reason to change my mind. But you will have to answer for your crimes. Poaching on a royal nature preserve is a pretty serious offense."

"I didn't even know this was where we were going when I signed up."

"Well, that's on you. But try saving it for the magistrate, huh?"

"Magistrate?"

Val grabbed him by the vest and hoisted him to his feet.

"Yeah. You're definitely going to jail."

CHAPTER 7

A short while later, Val found herself traipsing through the dense, muddy paths of the jungle.

The dragon slung to her back occasionally let out a high-pitched howl.

"Yeah, yeah."

The wailing continued as she soldiered on.

It took some time, but eventually, there was a return scream, much louder and deeper than the call from the baby. Trees shook, branches rattled, leaves were knocked loose and fluttered to the ground.

"Okay, seems like we found it."

She knelt down and let the straps of the backpack slip off her shoulders. She swung the bag around and set it on the floor before her before loosening the latches near the top and helping the squirming scaly creature wriggle free.

She could feel the ground shaking even before she was able to spot the fully-grown dragon slowly stomping its way through the trees in the distance.

Another appeared beside it, then another.

Val gestured for the baby to go towards them.

"Go on."

It stared up at her.

She gave it a gentle nudge.

"Go."

It rubbed its head against her hand and licked her

faceplate.

"Oh, no. I've got enough pets at home. There's no room for a dang dragon. Sure, you're cute and little now, but you'll be getting a ton bigger very soon."

The howling from the adult dragons grew fiercer.

"Get going. Your new family sounds impatient."

The little dragon shrieked back and scuttled off into the jungle.

The larger dragons looked down at it with wonderment, their screams growing more high-pitched and synced. The young one started to imitate the sound as best it could.

Val smiled beneath her helmet, turned, and followed her footprints back the way she came.

Val entered the cockpit of her ship and lifted the Crown, causing the armor that encased her body to unweave and disappear. The metal plating, the weapons-proof undersuit, all retracted like magic as the Crown itself shrank down from the full-faced plate to a normal-sized piece of royal headwear. The symbol of her station and source of the enchanted armor clung to her head still, held in place by some unseen – unknowable – force.

Beneath she wore a dark-colored bodysuit and heavy boots, along with the rigging around her chest, shoulders, and back that held her weaponry.

Her platinum hair was all pulled up towards the top of her head, piled into a thick, heavy braid that worked its way down her back.

The flight deck itself was intended for only a single pilot; while there were extra chairs built in, all were retracted and folded away, leaving Val's seat centered in front of the glowing, multilevel control console.

The jungle trees and vines whipped vertically past the forward view port as the ship lifted up. She was quickly in the sky and reaching for the overhead comms system.

"Hey, Bontu?"

There were several moments of dead air before a voice came from the other end.

"There you are."

"Yup, here I is."

"Where have you been?" Bontu's voice was deep enough to cause a bit of rumbling in the connection. "No one's heard from you in days."

"I've had some stuff to take care of," she said.

"That's not going to be good enough for Jenneca."

She leaned back in her chair.

"I'm aware. I thought I could sneak off and enjoy the birth of my newest dragon, but when I got to Ilmar I found the conservation warden prepping the mom and egg for transfer to some poachers. My guess is whatever tranquilizers he used caused her to birth early. And it turns out to be some of our own people. We're going to need a new warden and conservation transport teams, by the by. The idiot went and overdosed the mom on tranquilizers and then torched the enclosure system. I spent days getting everything back in order and waiting for the poachers to show up to catch them red-handed. Which, I'm aware, bumps me right up against the timetable. And that reminds me, have a contingent of guards ready when I land to transfer some prisoners."

"You took prisoners?" Bontu asked.

"As many as I could."

"I'm not sure I approve."

"Well, one benefit of being queen, I don't need the guardian's approval for just about anything."

"You know you've been queen for the better part of two decades now," Bontu said. "You can probably stop explaining the benefits of it every time you do anything."

"That's as much for me as anyone. I still spent more of my life not being queen than being queen at this point."

"And what should I tell Jenneca? Should we postpone the

ceremony?"

"No, she shouldn't postpone. She's been waiting for this for years. I'm sure she doesn't want to have to wait any longer."

"And I'm pretty sure she wants her mother there with her."

"It's not like I'm not trying."

She watched as, once out of the planet's atmosphere, a spatial anomaly opened in front of her vessel. The craft glided right in and the fold in space closed behind her.

CHAPTER 8

Val's luxurious cruiser cut through the clouds above the capital city of Olivert and came to a rest on the circular landing platform outside the royal palace.

Before the craft had fully come to a stop Val had popped an emergency hatch on the cockpit's side. She was met by her cousin Bontu, a hairy hulk of a man in a cleanly pressed black uniform with white piping along the jacket.

With Bontu came a contingent of armed palace guards in black and red uniforms who moved towards the rear of the ship.

"She's waiting," said Bontu.

He and the queen hurried towards the stone catwalk that would take them to the nearest tower of the palace.

"Of course she is," said Val. "She's a teenager. It's her job to be impatient with her mother. Remember, as soon as she hit puberty, I'm not allowed to do anything right in her eyes."

"You've got blood on your clothes," he said.

They made it inside and took a right down one of the wideset corridors.

"These aren't the clothes I'm wearing to the ceremony." Val checked the timepiece at her waist. "Damn. I probably don't have time for a shower."

"You barely have time to change."

"Yeah, I just have to run back to my quarters and grab a fresh dress."

"Toni's waiting in the training circle."

"That's handy."

"Anything else you need?"

Val caught a glimpse of her reflection in a passing window.

"Ugh. I look a mess," she said. "I'll never hear the end of it."

"Anything you need that can be accomplished between here and there?"

"Do you have any cleaning wipes?"

"No."

"No, of course not. My braid could probably use some tightening."

Bontu slowed his pace just for a moment to get behind her. His thick fingers went to work, pulling on her hair and delicately weaving any loose strands back into formation.

Their path soon brought them into contact with a pair of teenagers stood in the hallway. Both tan, the boy wore a red suit not dissimilar in style to those of Bontu and the palace guard, while the girl wore an elegant gown.

The two of them were swept up in Val and Bontu's unbroken stride.

"There you are," said the girl, Jenneca. "Jeez. I was worried you were going to be late."

"You literally can't do this without me," said Val, "so whenever I show up, I'm on time."

"Technically we can't do this without the thing on your head," said the boy, Donnie.

"Well, we're kind of a package deal at this point." Val looked to her daughter. "I am sorry I had you worried, honey. But you'll be fine. There's nothing to it."

"You never had to go through this. How would you know?" Jenneca asked.

"It's basically putting on a hat," said Val. "You can handle that, right?"

"If not, I'm literally right here," said Donnie.

Jenneca shot him a sideways glance. "Shut up, Donnie."

"Jenneca," said Val.

"What?"

"Be nice to your brother."

"Your brother who's not at all nervous and could handle this responsibility, no problem," Donnie added.

Val looked to him.

"You know she's not wrong about you needing to shut it. Of course you're not nervous. No one is even going to be looking at you. You don't even have to be here."

"It would look improper if I wasn't here for my sister's big day."

"Oh, now you're worried about being proper?" Jenneca asked.

They passed a servant girl in the hallway.

Val smiled to her.

"Hey, Naoke."

The girl bowed her head. She was trim, with dark features: barely older than the royal children.

"My queen."

"Mom already knows the new girl's name?" Donnie asked his sister.

"I think she's worked here for about a year."

"Whatever, I can't keep track of them all."

"I think you tried to sleep with her once."

"I said what I said."

The royal training room had changed very little since Val's youth. The circular structure, of course, remained the same, but so did the markings on the floor, the weapons racks and exercise equipment pushed against the walls.

The stability of its appearance was undoubtedly owed in part to its unchanging master, the tall, broad, sleeveless giant called Trainer.

"I still don't get why she gets the Crown," Donnie said to his mother.

"She's not 'getting the Crown,' this is just the first time

she's allowed to train with it on."

"It's still stupid. How come she gets it and I don't? Just because she's older?" Donnie asked.

"Yes," Val said. "Exactly. That's the way the order of succession works."

"This isn't fair."

"Life's not fair. I've taught you that."

"Since I was three."

"I'm sure I mentioned it before that. You were probably just too young to remember anything earlier."

"But she didn't do anything to deserve it." The pitch of Donnie's voice crept up just slightly. "It's not my fault she was born five days earlier than me."

"It's not my fault, either," said Jenneca.

"That's kind of my point," Donnie replied.

"My point is, stopping whining about it," Jenneca said.

Donnie turned to Val.

"Mom."

"She's right," Val said. "This is a big day for her. Don't ruin it."

"Seriously?"

"You're a prince of Kaia," Val said. "You'll have plenty of important days of your own. This is Jenneca's."

"Are we ready to begin?" Trainer asked.

Val shot Donnie a side-eyed glance.

"We are," she said. "But, it's up to Jenneca."

"Yes." Jenneca took a breath. "Yeah, I'm ready."

The Crown case rose from the floor, a solid, ornate pillar with a clear box at the top. The transparent section split along unseen edges and blossomed open like a flower.

Val quickly plucked the Crown from her head and set it atop the pedestal.

"Sorry," she said. "Ceremony, tradition, right."

Jenneca hesitantly stepped towards it.

From the far side of the column, Trainer's eyes locked onto her as she shuffled nearer to the display.

"Go on."

The young woman's hands shook a bit as she reached out for the Crown, grasping it gently with her fingertips.

Val looked on, a prideful grin stretched across her face.

Jenneca nervously smiled as she placed the Crown against her head.

She let go.

Her heart jumped at the loud clanging of metal against stone.

The Crown sat on the floor.

Jenneca stared at the others. They stared back, not moving to so much as breathe for the moment.

"What does this mean?" she asked.

BOOK 2: NEVA

CHAPTER 1

Morning crept over the town of Hermber, located just a few hundred miles from the capitol on Kaia.

Shops opened on its quiet streets as citizens hurried to their jobs or their school.

The morning rush was long past – but lunch not yet arrived – when the manager of the café noticed a disturbance outside their windows. He gave the pair of girls behind the counter a concerned look before stepping out to investigate.

"Where's he going?"

Were it not an off day, the girl was young enough that she'd be in school.

Instead, she got a shrug from her coworker and the pair of them returned to lazily pretending to clean and organize behind the cabinets of baked goods.

She moved around to get a look at a countertop display and caught a glimpse of the manager stood outside, worriedly interacting with a contingent of people in military uniforms.

Not just military: black and red.

"Holy shit. Are those palace guards?"

"Ooh, Neva. What'd you do?" her coworker chided.

Neva scoffed. "Shut up."

The bell above the door chimed out as the manager reentered the building. It was still reverberating by the time he'd reached the counter.

His voice wobbled a bit. "Neva, there're some people

outside who'd like to speak with you."

Her coworker's head snapped up.

"Oh, shit, really? God, I was just joking."

"What'd I do?" asked Neva.

The manager's head swayed back and forth.

"They just said they want to talk to you."

"I didn't... I mean, I've never been in serious trouble before. What do I do?"

"You can't run," her coworker said. "Not from the palace guard."

"So what do I do?"

Her manager's face went flat.

"I think you go talk to them."

The morning sun had not yet finished its job of warming the air when Neva stepped outside, still bedecked in her blue apron and black work clothes.

She timidly approached the waiting contingent of guards.

"Hi. Uh, can I ask what I did?"

One of them looked down on her.

"It's nothing you did, miss." He placed a device against her exposed arm. "This should only take a second."

"What is that?" Her voice jumped enough to attract attention from the few passersby on the street. "What's going on?"

The device let out a "boop." A red indicator light flashed into the guardsman's face.

He tapped his ear.

"We have a positive ID."

Tears welled up in Neva's eyes.

"What does that mean?"

An armored convoy approached the palace, heading

through the gates and up the path to the main entrance.

Other than the roar of the engines of the heavy craft, the trip had been made in absolute silence. Not a word had passed between Neva and the suited royal guardsman, to say nothing of the armed troopers that dotted the vehicles both inside and out.

Neva found herself sat in a nondescript room on one side of a small table. The chair opposite her was empty.

Overall the room was poorly lit, with the few dim fixtures giving off a sickly cast.

The chair, while spartan in appearance, was surprisingly comfortable. Even interrogations in the palace were done with style, she figured.

And yet she found herself shifting uneasily, unable to quite maintain a stillness.

After some time – she couldn't say how long, perhaps a few minutes, perhaps the better part of an hour – the door finally reopened. Due to conditions within the room, the figure that entered was naught but a dark silhouette and indistinct for just a moment before Neva's eyes adjusted.

"Hello, Neva."

Neva's last shift nearly toppled her from her seat.

"Oh, my God. Queen Valentina."

Val approached the table with an easy smile on her face.

"You're in the royal palace. It doesn't make sense for you to be surprised to see me here."

Neva's mouth was dry.

"Nothing about today has made sense."

"I suppose that's fair."

The chair made a loud screech as Val pulled it out and sat herself down opposite the younger woman.

Neva bowed her head.

"My queen."

"Don't. Don't do that."

Neva swallowed hard despite the lack of saliva.

"Isn't it considered proper?"

"It is, but, just, don't, okay?"

"As you wish. My queen."

Val sighed.

"I take it no one's told you why you're here?"

"No one's said much of anything to me."

"Okay. That's fine. That's good. I'd rather be the one to tell you. You ready for a story?" Neva stared at her. "Okay, so, when I first became queen, I was made aware, keenly aware, I might even say painfully aware, that one of my duties would be to propagate the royal bloodline. You get that, right?"

Neva nodded enthusiastically.

"Right," Val said. "Now, we had wars to fight, armies to lead, etcetera, so I couldn't be pregnant. It just wouldn't have been practical. So, a handful of women were chosen as surrogates to carry my babies. The first one to give birth had a girl."

"Yes, I know." Neva's words became rapid. "Princess Jenneca."

Val sighed again. There was something different about the tone this time, more wistful than impatient.

"No. Well, yes. But, no. I named her Jenneca, but, that isn't the girl I raised."

"I don't understand."

"It was you."

CHAPTER 2

D ays earlier, as the queen, members of the royal family, and assorted associates and attendants had gathered to watch Princess Jenneca don the Crown of the Ten Point Star for the very first time, something unexpected happened.

Jenneca stared at the Crown, still sitting on the floor.

"What…"

Val turned to her retinue.

"Bontu, get everyone out. Out of this wing. Clear the floor. Not a word of this to anyone until we figure this out."

Her gregarious cousin and guardian nodded and headed for the door.

Jenneca looked up at her mother, her confusion turning to panic.

"Mom. What does this mean?"

The queen wrapped her arms around her child and held tight.

"I don't know, baby. But it's going to be alright."

The queen typically didn't make use of much technology in her sitting room. It was a simple setting, classically decorated. To bring in modern accoutrements felt like a betrayal of the old world aesthetic that had been carefully preserved there.

But, it was where Val went when she felt uneasy, and she

had work to do.

She sat at the computer terminal contained therein, usually disguised within a wooden bureau. Bontu was nearby, hunkered into an overstuffed armchair.

"This doesn't make sense," Val said. "Jenneca is of the blood. The Crown should speak to her."

Bontu shrugged.

"Maybe."

"Maybe?" Val turned to him. "What do you mean, maybe?"

"This isn't the same Crown that's been passed down from generation to generation."

"No, it's four of the Crowns that have been passed down from generation to generation."

"But maybe bonding them changed something," said Bontu. "Or maybe Dayo damaged them with that Destroyer armor? I don't know. I'm just throwing stuff out there."

"Well, we can't just sit here throwing out theories. We've got to figure out how to test them."

"Would Trainer know?"

Val gave her head a sullen shake.

"No, his order lost their magic ages ago. None of the mages in the empire would understand the Crowns." Her face became stern. "Bring my other children here."

Bontu shrugged again and stood.

"Alright."

The royal infirmary, though nondescript from without, took up a sizeable portion of its own wing of the castle. It was, plainly, the most advanced medical facility in the empire.

Within, it was well-stocked and staffed, containing surgical wards, examination rooms, and research facilities that would be the envy of any physician or academic in the known galaxy.

It was though, above all, a hospital, and maintained a

regular medical care ward to the highest of standards.

Not a speck of dust would go unscrutinized in the full vivid light, and that dedication to sterility was applied down to the microscopic level.

Val entered into the general examination room, accompanied by Bontu and a contingent of guards.

Dr. Boon was one of the senior general practitioners. He kept an office very near to the space that the queen's retinue noisily stormed through.

Upon the scion reaching his office, he stood swiftly from behind his desk and bowed.

"My queen."

Val glared at him.

"Is, um, is everything alright?" he asked.

"I'm not sure. You know, today was supposed to be Jenneca's crowning day."

"Oh?" Boon asked. "I hadn't heard. We don't really keep up with those sorts of things around here."

Val clutched her teeth and raised an eyebrow. "Do you know what happened?"

"How could I?"

"The Crown wouldn't speak to her."

"What?"

She stepped closer.

"The Crown. Wouldn't speak. To her."

"I heard you, I'm just not sure..."

"The Crown should speak to anyone of the royal blood. To be sure, I had all my other children try it on. And it spoke to each of them. But they're not next in line in the order of succession."

"My queen, I..."

"So, I wondered, what could have gone wrong? Anyone of the blood should be able to wear the Crown. The only reasonable conclusion is that, somehow, my oldest daughter isn't my child."

"I..." The single stammered syllable was swallowed somewhere in his throat.

"We got a portable scanner to verify. So, I asked myself,

how could that be? She was born to a surrogate, so my first thought was that, maybe the surrogate had been pregnant without realizing before my egg was implanted in her."

Dr. Boon quickly nodded.

"It's possible…"

"But then I realized that, there's no way the royal physician would miss that. On her first health scan. On every single physical, every examination, every checkup for the last sixteen years." Val stepped closer still. "I mentioned we did our own scan of her, yeah?"

Boon swallowed hard and nodded, slowly this time.

"It was the first time in her life anyone but you checked her DNA. And you know what we found."

Dr. Boon found his eyes unable to continue contact with his queen's.

"She's not my daughter. Not biologically, anyway. And the DNA scan we did today? It looks nothing like the ones you've had on record for sixteen years. You've been her doctor all her life. We've pretty well worked out the 'what.' Now what I want from you, is the 'why.'"

"I – I – I…"

Val moved her head to catch his gaze.

"Hm?"

"I'm sorry." He quickly reached into his desk and grabbed a palm-sized device.

Val moved to stop him, but was seized by the arms and tugged away as the doctor pressed the button located in the device's center. In a quick flash of energy, all that was left of him was a wisp of crimson vapor.

"What the hell?" Val asked.

Bontu released her.

The queen dropped to one knee beside the scorched stain on the carpeting where the doctor had only moments earlier stood.

She looked up at Bontu, her mouth hanging open, desperation in her eyes.

◆ ◆ ◆

Val did her best to remain calm as she finished relaying all of this to Neva.

"It took us a little bit of digging after that. We might never really know the how and, more importantly, the why. But we found you."

"Found me." Neva's voice stumbled from her lips, barely projecting. "Because I'm..."

Val placed her hand on the girl's.

"You... you were supposed to be Jenneca. Obviously, you're not. You're Neva. But, if you hadn't been switched, yeah, you would have been raised as Princess Jenneca. The firstborn daughter and heir to the Crown."

Neva tried to make eye contact.

"So, you're my mom?"

"I'm... sort of, yes. It gets complicated, doesn't it? The Nuws, they raised you well, didn't they?"

"Yeah. They... I mean..."

"You're a teenager." Val gave her a warm smile. "I get it. You can't say that your parents did a good job."

"Could you've?"

"I didn't have to worry about that. When I was your age, I had no idea who my parents were."

"Really?"

"You're not a fan of opera, are you?"

"No. Why?"

"They tell the history of my... of our family. When I was your age, I was in hiding as a palace attendant. I was just about to enter the military academy."

"Oh."

They sat in silence.

"So, what happens now?" Neva finally asked.

"I don't know. Which is kind of standard for me, actually. I really wish something about my reign would go according to the normal procedures, you know? But it seems like the whole thing has been detonating tradition and having to make everything up as I go. I think it's safe to say, your life as you knew it is over."

"How come?" Neva asked.

"We won't be able to keep this a secret. Right now, you're one of maybe four living people who know the truth. But word will get out. You can't go back to your old life with people knowing who you are. People will treat you differently. You'll be a target for enemies of the crown."

"Oh."

"Your parents will be welcome to come live here with you."

"I'm going to live in the palace?" Neva asked.

"Of course. It's by far the safest place."

"Oh my…"

"What?" Val asked. "Is there something wrong? I mean, besides the obvious."

Neva looked up at her.

"It's… my job."

"Your job?" Val cocked her head to the side.

"The palace guard found me when I was at work. I got pulled away."

"I don't think you need to worry about a part-time job anymore."

"But I kind of left my coworkers hanging."

Val smiled.

"You know, I think my brother would've liked you."

Neva tried to smile back.

"Hey, you know what would be kind of funny?" Val asked.

"Hm?"

"Just leave them hanging. Don't even go back and tell them what's going on. Let them wonder until… well, until word gets out, at least."

"Wouldn't that be kind of mean?" Neva asked.

"Yes, but also kind of funny."

The door to the room opened again. A royal attendant,

clad all in red, ushered a middle-aged couple in and shut the door behind them.

Neva gave them a half-hearted smile.

"Hi mom. Hi dad."

"Hello," Val said warmly.

They bowed.

"My queen," the pair said nearly in unison.

Mrs. Nuw looked to her daughter.

"Neva, honey, what's going on?"

"Some soldiers showed up to my work..." Her dad nervously tugged on his shirt sleeve.

Val looked to Neva.

"Would you like to be the one to tell them?" she asked.

"Me?"

"It might be easier coming from you."

"Alright." She rose from the table and headed towards her parents. "Well, we're not supposed to worry about missing work anymore."

Val stepped out into the hallway, leaving the three of them in private. Bontu was there to meet her. The two of them watched through the small window on the door as a look of shock and confusion overcame Neva's parents. Things came to a head as the three of them broke down in tears and held onto one another.

"The doctor couldn't have been working alone," said Val.

"I'll get my people on it," Bontu said, "but, I mean, that trail's sixteen years cold by now.'

"I know. But we have to try. Someone has messed with my family."

"I know. We'll do whatever we can."

CHAPTER 3

L ike all of the royal chambers, Jenneca's room was lavishly appointed. Every fixture, every bit of molding, was just a bit more ornate than first glance would belie. She'd decorated it up a bit with her own sensibilities. Pictures of her family were dotted across her desk, pictures of her friends surrounded the vanity, portraits of her favorite singers and athletes adorned the walls.

As was the case with all the bedrooms assigned to the family, it was nestled away at the core of the wing. No direct access to the outside world meant no direct sunlight. It had been decided this way long ago for the security of the residents, though few could recall such a time as the precautions were necessary given the advanced state of defenses embedded into the castle over the centuries. Still, the bedrooms were what they were, and so the light, however clean and clear the fixtures could project, wasn't quite natural.

Like most rooms in the castle, it was large and round. The bed, also large and round, was set in the middle of it all, layered in fanciful pillows and covers.

Jenneca sat there, hugging her knees, her blankets and linens tossed off to one side.

There came a knock on the door. Val didn't wait for a response before entering.

"Hey," she said.

Jenneca didn't respond.

"Uh, the, um, the other girl and her family are here," Val said. "I didn't know if you were ready to meet them."

"You mean your daughter," said Jenneca.

Val was quickly at Jenneca's side, squishing down into a seat on the plush mattress beside her.

"Jenn, she's – yes, she's my daughter. But so are you."

Val tried to put an arm around Jenneca. She shrugged it off and turned away.

"I know this is hard," Val said. "But I raised you. Nothing can change that."

No response was forthcoming.

"Do you remember when you were six and you got the Tymerian flu?" Val asked.

"Not really."

"Oh."

"I know I almost died, and got the best medical care in the kingdom. Because people thought I was a princess."

"And I was by your bed, all day and night, until you were well enough to go back to school. Did you know that was the week of the Jasomony Peace Treaty conference?"

Jenneca's head spun to one side to look back at her.

"What?"

"I was supposed to be there. But my child was sick. I needed to be with you. To be there for you. I couldn't... I sent Bontu instead."

"You sent Bontu?" Jenneca asked. "To negotiate a peace treaty?"

"In hindsight, it's not the most obvious thing. But he came back with a signed treaty. And two more wives. The point is, nothing was more important to me than you. Nothing. That hasn't changed just because of some DNA scan."

"It's not just some DNA scan," Jenneca said. "I can't wear the Crown."

"I know."

"I've worked my whole life for that."

"I know. I remember when you were growing up, every

Mother's Day gift was somehow Crown-themed."

Jenneca gave a sad chuckle.

"I was a little obsessed."

"Yeah. Not as obsessed as you were with that boy Mrock in your writing class in eighth grade."

"Oh, my God, mooooom…"

"See? I can still embarrass you like only a mom can."

"Ugh."

"I know. You hate it when I'm right."

"Bleghk."

Val patted her leg.

"But, look, as hard as this is, we're going to have to get used to having Neva and her parents around. I know it won't be easy, but I hope you can get along with her. And, if her parents are anything like me, I'm sure they'd like to get to know you."

"Yeah."

Val rose up from the bedding.

"They're going to be dining with us in the grand hall tonight. I hope you'll be there. But if you're not ready yet, I'll totally understand."

She gave her daughter one last effort at a smile before leaving the room.

"Hi, I'm Val." The queen took Mr. and Mrs. Nuws each warmly by the hand and gave each of their arms a shake. "We met briefly earlier."

"Yes," said Mrs. Nuws, "we know who you are, my queen."

"Right, I just thought we should get to know one another a bit. Since you'll be living here and all."

"I still can't believe we're in the castle," Mr. Nuws said. "We never dreamed of this."

Val smiled.

"I bet you also never dreamed that you were raising a princess."

"No," said Mrs. Nuws. "We… ever since the day we brought her home from the hospital, we loved her like our own."

"And I've loved Jenneca. I don't expect that to change. I'm not going to take her away from you. I hope my reputation as queen would never make me out to be that cruel."

"No, of course not, my queen," said Mr. Nuws.

Val sighed.

Mrs. Nuws looked around the grand dining hall. It was not so crowded that she wouldn't be able to identify each occupant.

"Um, and where is the princess?"

"Probably in her room, I would guess," said Val. "This has all been very hard on her. Not only finding out the truth about her birth, but now losing what she'd thought was her birthright."

The large wooden doors nearby slowly crept open.

An older couple, dressed stylishly in robes, entered. The man held to a leash at the other end of which was a large wolf hound of some sort.

"Hi, everyone," said Jason. "Sorry we're late. This little guy here's not as frisky as he used to be. Is he?"

He bent down and scratched John under the chin. John looked up contentedly.

"Oh, my God," Mrs. Nuw gasped. She nudged her daughter with her elbow. "It's the royal grands."

"Who?" Neva asked.

"The… the grands," her mother whispered. "They're Queen Valentina's adopted parents."

"She wasn't adopted."

"No, she adopted them."

"Huh?"

Catherine Hammond approached them and offered her hand.

"Hello."

Mrs. Nuw's head dipped subserviently.

"Hello, Grand'ma."

Neva gave a weak wave.

"Hi."

"You must be Neva." The warmth of Catherine's smile was infectious.

"Yeah."

"Welcome. I know this must be a hard time for you."

"Yes. It is. And thank you."

Catherine looked to Mrs. Nuw.

"And you're her mother?"

"Yes, I am."

"Well, welcome to you, too. I'm sure you'll see me and my husband doddering around the castle. For a little while longer yet."

A girl in red, not much younger than Neva, if at all, approached their small grouping.

"Grand'ma!"

She threw her arms around Catherine.

"Sweety, we have guests."

"Of course." She held out her hand to Neva and her mother. "Hi. I'm Sanke."

"Of course. We... ah..." Mrs. Nuw took her offered hand. "I'm shaking hands with a princess."

"You get used to it very quickly," said Catherine. "After a bit they're just family."

"Uh, hi," Sanke said to Neva. "I guess, um, you're my older sister."

"God, that's weird to think of," said Neva. "But, hi. Sorry. I just..."

"Yeah."

Catherine felt pressed to interject.

"Do you have any other brothers or sisters?" she asked Neva.

"No. No, I'm an only child. Or, was."

"We had trouble conceiving," said Mrs. Nuw. "Neva was our little miracle. But, um..."

"I know, it's a strange situation, dear," said Catherine. "I'm intent on looking at the bright side. Our family just got a little bigger."

Donnie stood apart from any of the small groupings of people engaged in conversation. No one seemed to pay him any mind and he was happy to return the favor.

Val pattered towards her oldest son.

"Donnie, you've been awful quiet tonight. That's not like you."

"Mm-hmm."

"You're not even going to speak to your sister?"

"Which one do you suggest I address, mother?"

"Oh, don't do that."

"Do what, mother?"

"Address me as 'mother.' You know it's creepy."

"I'm not sure I follow, mother."

"Whatever. You can at least speak to Sanke and Joseph, and your grands."

"Surely, mother."

Val scoffed, rolled her eyes, and sauntered off.

Donnie looked towards the rest of the gathering. Sanke was conversing with Neva; Joseph stood nearby Jason and John.

He almost took a step towards them, but took notice of the girl, Naoke, among the servants in attendance. Balancing a tray, she deftly made her way towards the service entrance.

Donnie followed closely behind.

The main doors to the dining hall swung open, both, as far as their wide metal hinges would allow.

The room fell silent.

Jenneca's face, already a bright shade, flushed.

"I'm not, um, I didn't miss supper, did I?"

The room breathed a collective sigh of relief.

Val approached her and ruffled her hair.

"No, sweetie, you're right on time. Well, about five or ten minutes early. Maybe you should go say hi to..."

"The other me?"

"I was going to say 'Neva,' since that's her name."

"Duly noted."

She walked over to her counterpart. The pair was given a wide berth by the other guests.

"Hi," said Jenneca.

"Hi."

"I'm Jenneca."

"I know who you are."

"Oh, well then..."

"I didn't mean it like that. I'm sorry. But everyone in the empire knows who you are."

"Weird that they're all wrong then, huh?"

"What do you mean?"

"I'm not really Princess Jenneca, am I?"

"Well, I'm not."

"So, what, there just is no Princess Jenneca now?" Jenneca asked.

"Well we both can't be Neva Nuw."

"This is messed up."

"Yeah. Definitely," said Neva.

CHAPTER 4

Bontu entered the palace communications room in search of his queen. There he found her, sat on a console beside the holo-transcriber. Stood in the transcriber, an angular glowing pad with thin rails running across the front, was the newest addition to the royal family.

"What's going on?" he asked.

"We reached a compromise," said Val.

"On what?"

"Hi. It's Neva. I, um... I'm not going to be able to come into work anymore. No, I can't say anything more than that. Okay, uh, bye. Have a good, you know, life."

Neva clicked the transcriber off and stepped back.

Val burst out laughing. Neva was able to join in a bit.

"That felt weird," she said.

"Hey, sometimes in life you've gotta make your own fun," said Val. She looked to her cousin. "What did you need, Bontu?"

"Everything's been prepared," he said.

"Good." Val strode to his side and the pair of them walked out of the room. Val poked her head back in the door. "You coming, or...?"

"Oh," said Neva. "I didn't realize... I mean..."

Val's mouth flattened and her eyes widened.

"Okay." Neva hurried to catch up.

"We have something to decide on." Val sat before her children and adopted family members in the royal sitting room. "And it's not going to be pleasant. But we need to decide on it as a family."

"Then what's Trainer doing here?" Donnie asked.

"Your mother asked me to be here," Trainer said.

"I did," said Val. "Because Trainer's like family to us."

"He's like family, but he's not family." Donnie, sprawled out and taking up just a bit too much room on the side sofa, nodded towards Jenneca. "And neither is she."

Val's tone sharpened. "That is more than enough of that, young man. Do you understand me?"

"Yes."

"Good. I never want to hear another word like that out of you, ever again. No matter what happens, Jenneca is your sister. I raised you two together."

Donnie burst out with a laugh.

"You barely raised us."

"It's this sort of thing, this is why we have such a problem," Val said.

Jenneca looked to Donnie.

"What is wrong with you?" she asked.

"Nothing. I can wear the Crown just fine."

"Out," Val said pointedly.

"Beg pardon?" her son asked.

"You heard me. Get out. I said no more of that talk, and you deliberately disobeyed me, so you leave."

"What about our 'family meeting?'"

"You can be part of those when you've decided you can act like part of the family." She pointed towards the door. "Out."

Donnie sneered as he got up and left, slamming the door shut behind him.

Tension filled the room as the others watched him go.

Jenneca was the first to break it.

"God, he's such a little jerk."

"I won't argue too strongly with you, but he's still your

brother." Val rose up and started pacing. "Which is what makes this decision even harder."

"What decision?" Jenneca asked.

"Who gets the Crown," her mother said. "Who gets the throne. I mean, normally, it's cut and dry. The firstborn is next in line. But, we thought you were the firstborn, so we've spent the last 16 years preparing you for something that, you know, you can't do."

Jenneca's gaze fell to the floor.

"It's not your fault." Val tried to give her the briefest of smiles, a futile act considering Jenneca's eyeline never lifted. "But, by all rights, Neva should get the Crown. But she's a stranger. She hasn't been raised for this."

Jenneca didn't look up.

"Neither were you."

"I know." Val nodded solemnly as she sank back into her chair. "But this time, we have a choice. If Neva's deemed not fit for the Crown, then it should go to the next in the line of succession. Which, given the nature of the law, would be Donnie."

"Well, we don't know that Neva's unfit, right?" Jenneca asked.

"No," said Val. "But if she turns out to be good for it, how will Donnie react? Is it fair to him, when he's trained all his life as your backup, to give it to someone else now that you need a backup?"

Jenneca's eyes shot up.

"Who cares about what's fair to him?"

"Jenn..."

"She has a point," said Trainer. "Your primary concern should be to the kingdom, not sparing your son's feelings."

"That's probably true," Val said.

"That's why you have Trainer here," said Jenneca.

"No, we have Trainer here as a witness for the council," said Val. "These are weird times. While succession doesn't require their approval, they want to be kept abreast of any discussions."

"And you're okay with that?" Jenneca asked.

"Not really," said Val. "But we have to pick our battles. And I am cool with having Trainer here, even if he's here as a snitch."

"Come on," said Trainer.

"I'm just teasing you."

"I know, but, still, spare an old man's feelings."

"Okay, can I say something?" Jenneca asked.

"That's why you're here," said Val.

"Well, we only need to have a succession plan for if you die. So, if you don't die for a while, do we really need to worry about it?"

"Unfortunately, we do," said Trainer. "That's why a succession plan is put in place. For the eventuality that the monarch might become unable to dispense their duties. For whatever reason."

"Okay, but what if, I mean, you could name Neva as your successor, right?" Jenneca asked. "And start her training right away. So, by the time she's needed, she'll be ready."

"She's already well behind," Trainer said.

Val looked to him.

"So was Joe."

Trainer took a breath.

"And look how that turned out."

They heard a slight clinking coming from the door. Val whipped around the see Naoke stood there, a tray in her hands.

The attendant quickly vanished back into the hallway.

"Wait," said Val, "was she here the whole time?"

The others looked between themselves and shrugged.

Val rose up out of her seat and ran after the servant.

The adjacent hallway was virtually empty save for Val and Naoke, who'd made it a fair distance away by the time Val left the room.

"Naoke, wait up." It was little problem for Val to catch her. "God, you're a fast one, aren't you?"

"I... I'm sorry my queen. I didn't mean to intrude. I only...

I'm so sorry..."

"Whoa, hey, easy. Calm down. Breathe. It's fine. I mean, it's not, but it is what it is. No one outside of our family knows what we were discussing in there. So it can't get out, okay? Not even a little bit. You can tell no one, at all. Understood?"

Naoke nodded vigorously, her thick curly hair bouncing across her shoulders.

"Yes, my queen."

"I mean it. And if it does get out, well, you're the only one who wasn't invited into that room that knows so we'd know who we'd be looking for right away."

Naoke nodded again and swallowed hard.

"May I go now?"

"Yeah. Yeah, I think we were pretty much done in there anyway. As done as we're going to get for tonight." She turned and saw her family filing out of the sitting room. "And I guess I'm not the only one who thought that."

Catherine approached and patted her on the shoulder.

"I'm sorry, dear, but it seemed like we were all just a little too tired to be making good decisions tonight."

"You're probably right."

"That's why you keep me around, isn't it?"

Catherine gave her a wink before she, Jason, and John headed off.

CHAPTER 5

Jenneca made for her chambers following the meeting. For whatever reason, Donnie was headed back the way she was coming, still in full military dress.

The section of corridor where their paths intersected was quiet and dark. A narrow spiraling stairway lay off to one side, corkscrewing down into the castle's inner workings.

"Hello, Jenneca. If that is your real name."

"Of course it is. Don't be a dork."

He stood in her path.

"It's really not, though, if you think about it."

"Shut up."

"I'm just saying, your actual birth certificate lists you as Neva Nuw."

"Shut the hell up, nut-wipe."

"Okay, look, I'm going to be serious for a second."

"I don't care."

"Oh, 'cause that hurts."

"You've been a real asshole of a brother to me for sixteen years. I'm not going to give a shit what you have to say now."

He moved close to her. Too close. She could feel the uncomfortable moisture of his breath on her neck.

"But that's the thing, right? I'm not your brother. Not really."

"As much as it sucks, yeah, you are."

His hand darted out, taking hold of her arm.

"No, I'm not. And that's not necessarily a bad thing."

"Let go of me." Tried as she might, she couldn't break his grip.

His lip curled up.

"Things that were off-limits yesterday are suddenly on the table today."

"I said, let go...!"

His other hand went over her mouth.

"You are attractive, in your own way. It's almost understandable how someone could've mistaken you for royalty. I'd have chalked it up to good genes, but, well, now we know what kind of trash you really come from, don't we?"

After the tense few moments of thrashing, an idea finally struck her. Her teeth went down, into the flesh of her brother's hand.

The grunts of pain the action elicited convinced her to try her luck pulling away again. Still she was unable to wriggle free.

He finally relented his grip on her face only to force his hand between her legs. With his body he pressed her against the wall, his free hand undoing the front of his pants.

"Come on," he breathed. "We're young, pretty people."

"STOP IT!"

He grabbed her by the jaw and shoved her back into the cold stone. Had she not juked her head, his lips would have made contact with hers. Yet, as he worked her skirt up and pushed his leg between her thighs, she could not get away.

Finally, desperately, she let her knees give way and her legs buckle, violently thrashing to the ground.

She felt herself hit the first step, then another. They came in quick succession, Jenneca unable to stop her momentum as she plummeted downwards.

Donnie gave chase for a few steps before turning and sprinting away.

The workers in the room below dropped everything as the screaming princess tumbled into the room. They all rushed to her side.

"Oh, my God," one of them gasped.

"Princess, are you alright?" asked another.

"No. Get my mother, as fast as you can. Donnie attacked me. I think I broke something on the stairs. I need to see a doctor, and I need my mom."

As the workers began to rush off to carry out her instructions, Jenneca grabbed one by the skirt and held her back.

"Don't leave me."

The older attendant looked down at the bruised young woman, her wide eyes filling.

"Alright."

"And, please, if Donnie comes back, keep him away from me."

"The prince really did this."

Jenneca nodded.

CHAPTER 6

A short while later, Val strode purposefully down another palace hallway. Bontu and a handful of palace guards trailed closely behind.

"How do you know where he'll be?" Bontu asked.

"Because he's my son."

"Did you know your son was capable of this?"

The door to Donnie's chambers burst open.

Seated on the bed, Donnie bolted upright. He looked at the new arrivals with a stare of doe-eyed innocence.

"Mother."

Val remained motionless in the doorway while the palace guard swarmed around her and towards her son.

"What's going on? Is something wrong?" he asked.

The guards gripped him and shoved him towards the door.

Val was unmoved from her position.

"You assaulted a princess," she said coldly.

"I'm a prince!"

"Not anymore. You're being stripped of your title."

"And she is not my sister! She's nothing! I am of the blood!"

"It doesn't matter. What you did..." Her face reddened. "If you were anyone but my son, you'd be executed immediately."

"So what are you going to do with me?"

"You're being exiled."

"Exiled? To where?"

"It won't matter. A battalion is being sent with you. You'll be kept under house arrest."

"For..."

"For the rest of your life. You'll have no contact with anyone. They will make sure you stay in that house, and the galaxy stays safe from you. With lethal force, if necessary. This is the only kindness you'll get from me."

She stepped to one side.

"Kindness? You might as well kill me now!"

Val shook her head, her nostrils flaring at regular intervals.

"Where did I go wrong with you?"

"Where you went wrong was having other kids before me."

He gave no serious resistance as the guards dragged him off, out of the bedroom he'd occupied for as far back as his memory traveled.

Val stood in the room, immobilized.

Bontu gently placed a hand on her shoulder. She didn't react.

He left.

BOOK 3: THE HEIST

CHAPTER 1

Neva awoke in strange surroundings.

The curtains that encircled her bed had been neglected the previous night, leaving her to stare at the tall walls of the rounded room, set far from where she lay.

This was her room, she realized momentarily, and yet none of it felt hers. It was exquisitely decorated in the royal tradition, not a touch of her personality yet visible anywhere.

Rolling out from beneath her plush covers, she glanced down at her sleepwear. A simple top and trousers, and yet they were nicer than any clothes she'd ever before worn in her life.

She dangled her feet off the side of the bed, dipping them into a waiting pair of slippers. Her feet were still calloused from long days at the café; her joints still ached for the same reason.

Getting up and giving herself a stretch, she looked her reflection over in the mirror above the wash station. She scrubbed up, ran a comb through her hair, and went to the wardrobe to pick an outfit for the day.

Jenneca rolled out of her own bed and went to her sink. After scrubbing at the tear tracks beneath her eyes, she carefully applied her skincare routine.

Her clothing for the day – a black and red skirted uniform, somewhat militaristic in appearance – had been selected and laid out the night before.

She looked at the sigil on the breast and sighed before slipping the jacket on.

In one of many kitchenettes that dotted the palace, Jenneca finished brewing a caffeinated beverage and sat down with her mug and a plate: a fried roll and some grilled meat strips.

The particular kitchenette had been selected due to its out-of-the-way location. At this hour and in this location, the odds of being disturbed or indeed interacted with by anyone should have been extremely low.

Naoke entered, carrying a tray. She spotted Jenneca and quickly backtracked.

In one of the larger dining halls – not one of the finer ones where state dinners would be held, nor one of the public cafeterias where staff would take meals – Neva sat with her parents. From several platters of meat, eggs, and baked goods, she shoveled food onto her plate, then from the plate to her mouth.

"Honey, slow down, you'll choke," her mother warned.

"Nuh-uh. Carbo-loading."

"Pretty sure that's not how that works." Her father barely glanced up from his morning news pad.

"One way to find out."

Her parents shared a solemn look.

"We wanted, that is, we were hoping to have some time to talk before your training this morning," said her mother.

"'M not stopping you."

"Hon, please. This is serious business."

Neva finally swallowed and paused.

"So."

Her mother's voice became flat, ashen.

"We've barely spoken after the initial shock of finding out that, um, well…"

"I'm not your daughter?"

"No."

"Not ever," her father said. He'd already took his focus off his pad, but not set it aside. "You're our daughter in every way that matters."

"Uh-huh.

"Have you, I mean, do you spend any time thinking…" Her father choked up. "I'm sorry."

Her mother began to get weepy as well.

"You know, every parent always wants what's best for their child," her father said. "You're our child, but, do you wonder what it would have been like, if you hadn't…"

"Been switched at birth, you mean?" Neva asked.

He nodded.

"I don't know," she admitted. "It's hard to grasp. The whole idea. I'm more focused on what I do now, I guess. We can't ever go home, to the house where I grew up."

"We live in a castle now," said her mother. "That's not a bad trade-off."

Neva smiled just a bit.

"I don't know when I'll see my friends again."

"You'll make new friends."

"It's a big adjustment, but your mom's right. Anytime you move or make a big life change, you're always starting over."

"We've never made a big move before. We lived in that same house all my life."

"Well, we'd talked about moving a few times," said her mother. "Especially once you got older. We could always use a little more space."

Neva looked around at the high stone walls and wooden rafters that surrounded them.

"We've got tons of space now. The bed I slept on last night was bigger than my bedroom back home." She looked down. "I guess it's not home anymore."

"Home will always be wherever the three of us are together," her father said.

Neva looked at him.

"I can't believe you just said that."

"That was really corny, dear," said his wife.

"See, this is why I never try to sweet talk."

Naoke appeared in the doorway.

"Um, excuse me, my princess. Trainer has sent word that he's ready for you."

Neva patted her belly as she rose up from the table.

"Wishing I'd loaded up some more carbs, but, oh well. Here I go."

CHAPTER 2

Trainer waited, as patiently as he ever did. Jenneca stood off to his side, her arms folded. Her last memories of the training room were not pleasant ones. Being there again had her heart rate elevated.

Naoke appeared in the doorway and gestured inward. Neva entered. Naoke closed the doors on her way out.

Neva approached the pair.

"Hello, Trainer."

"Hello, Princess Neva."

"Oh, wow, I don't think I'll be used to that for a while."

"You will, though."

Neva pointed to Jenneca.

"Okay, but, why is Jenneca here?"

"My mom thought it might be helpful."

"Oh."

"I mean, I can go if..."

"It's fine, I mean..."

"Really."

"No. I just don't know what I'm supposed to be doing, and..."

"That's kind of why my mom wanted me here. I'm pretty much the only living person who's ever gone through the training."

"Really?" Neva asked.

"Yes," said Trainer.

"Queen Valentina, er, uh… still not sure what I should call her, but, your mom never… I mean, she's a great warrior."

"Yes, and she went through advanced military and special operative training," Trainer said. "But as she was a hidden heir, she was never formally trained in the use of the Crown."

"I can't wear the Crown, but I was still trained in the theories and prepared for, well, for what you're about to do," said Jenneca.

"And, wait, none of your other siblings did this?" Neva asked.

"Not completely," Jenneca said. "They've had basic combat training, so they're at a slightly more advanced step than you. Hopefully you can join them soon. Joseph and Sanke, I mean. But no one really expected them to need to step up, so I don't think they ever took it seriously."

"Oh. But I'm…"

"No one knows what the future holds," said Trainer. "And it's been a long time since I've had a new student. So, shall we begin?"

"Wait," Jenneca interjected, "you never asked me if I was ready to begin."

"Because your mother told me when to begin."

"Seriously?"

"As the queen, that is her right."

"But I'm a princess," said Jenneca. "Don't I have that same right?"

"In theory, I suppose, but it's not usual…"

"Begin."

"Are you serious?" Trainer asked.

"Yes, I'm serious. I'm ordering you to begin. Please." She looked to the other girl. "Sorry. This is probably going to hurt."

"What is?" Neva asked.

"All of it."

Neva's eyes bulged.

"I'll be up there." Jenneca pointed to the observation deck that encircled the upper portion of the training room. "Trainer, put her through the paces."

CHAPTER 3

A royal cruiser landed in an unkempt grassy field near a small, white house. The structure itself was uninspired: two stories, a porch, wooden covers over the windows.

The hatch of the ship opened. A single guard descended, shunting the former prince Donnie down the ramp.

"Okay, okay," Donnie whined. "No need to push."

"And yet…"

The guard gave him another shove as they crossed the yard.

No longer was he bedecked in the dress of a head of state, but instead wore simple, neutral garments. The shag of his hair was somehow already bordering on unkempt.

The front door opened and Donnie stumbled in, followed by the guard, who then shut it behind them.

"This is where you'll be spending the rest of your natural life," the guard announced.

"As opposed to my unnatural life?" Donnie looked around the place. Everything about it was functional, utilitarian. The furniture looked old but sturdy, the light fixtures slightly dim. Nothing was unclean or broken. The hardwood floors in each room had variously styled rugs protecting them. "God, what a dump."

"It's actually a pretty nice place."

"I grew up in a palace."

"Doesn't mean you have to be an oblivious little shit."

"Sorry, I'm sure this is, you know, nicer than your house."

"Yeah, but the nice thing about this place is, I can leave if I want to."

"Oh, haha. I can't help it if I have an appreciation for the finer things. I'm a prince of the crown."

"Kid, you ain't shit anymore. You've been stripped of your title, placed under house arrest, and you're gonna have round-the-clock guards from now on. And all of us know what you did and would just love the chance to ring your skinny little neck. You so much as make it out the front door without permission, we have the authority to put you down."

Donnie's face twisted into a thin smirk.

"Well, this is going to be fun."

"It better not be. The rest of us think you're getting off too easy as it is."

"Speaking of getting off, are there any women on this planet?"

The guard sneered at him.

"You really haven't learned a damn thing, have you?"

"I'm not... I meant prostitutes. Or, just women who like to have a good time."

"How are you going to pay for prostitutes? You don't have any money or access to the treasury. And how are you going to show women a good time? You're under house arrest. No drink, no drugs, no contraband of any kind. You get fed and you have a roof, that's about it."

"What about games?" Donnie asked.

"What about them?"

"Are there any games here? Or even a deck of cards? I've got to do something for however long I'm here."

"There's a small library on the other side of the house." The guard pointed.

"Sounds thrilling."

"Learn to fall in love with the written word."

Donnie trained his gaze upward as he ventured deeper

into the structure.

"Oh, I can see we're going to get along famously."

CHAPTER 4

Trainer stood near the middle of the training room, pacing in a tight circle to keep an eye on Neva. She sprinted around the room's exterior: soaked in sweat, a worryingly pale tone to her complexion.

He glanced down every so often at the timepiece in his hand.

"Alright," he announced, "that's enough."

Neva stopped running and shuffled towards him, sucking for air.

She doubled over and vomited.

"Sorry," she said.

"Well, it is what it is."

"Yeah, I may have done carbo-loading wrong."

"Unquestionably."

He handed her a bottle of water and a small towel.

"Sorry," she said again between gulps. "I'm sure none of your other students have puked from their training."

"You'd be wrong about that."

"Really?"

"My training is designed to condition a subject for combat as quickly as possible. I understand that it can be rather intense, especially for those who are, shall we say, unaccustomed to such strenuous activity."

"Did Queen Valentina ever vomit from training?"

"No."

"Never?"

"She was brought up in the military tradition. I seem to recall she once vomited prior to a training session, but that turned out to be food poisoning."

"And she still worked out?"

"She proceeded to run an eight-minute mile."

"I kind of hate her right now." She glanced at his closed hand. "Did I at least do it?"

"Do what?"

"Whatever you were timing."

"I was just establishing a baseline. You weren't against any goal."

"Oh."

Jenneca descended the stairs.

"Okay, I'm back," she said.

"You left?" Neva asked.

"Yeah, I got bored and went for a snack. From the smell, I take it we've reached the 'puking' phase of training."

"Yes," said Trainer.

"Gross. Maybe we move away from hand-to-hand stuff for a bit? At least until the floor is clean?" Jenneca went to the door and opened it just enough to poke her head out. "Naoke, can you get someone from sanitation in here?"

"Right away, princess."

"Thank you, Naoke."

Jenneca returned to Trainer and Neva.

"Now, shall we continue?" Trainer asked.

"Hold on," said Jenneca. "She just barfed."

"Her mother once barfed and put in a full workout."

"Maybe we need some assessment." She turned to Neva. "How are your archery skills?"

"I did it a few times at summer camp."

"And your swordsmanship?"

"Swordsmanship?"

"The use and operation of a bladed weapon," said Trainer.

"I know what it means. You guys know I was a waitress in

a café until a few days ago, right? We had a bread knife behind the counter I managed to cut myself on."

"Okay, this is... workable," said Jenneca.

"Of course it is," said Trainer. "Your mother trusts me to work it, as I have done countless times in my tenure here."

"My mom also asked me to get involved. And I have an idea."

"Deviation from the program tends to yield suboptimal results," Trainer stated.

"How would you know?" Jenneca asked. "Have you ever seriously tried it?"

She grabbed Neva by the sleeve and pulled her towards the door.

"Come on."

Trainer shook his head before following after.

"I see this ending poorly."

Soon after, a sky-flyer containing Trainer, Neva, Naoke, and Jenneca rocketed away from the castle, out over the plains away from Olivert. The speed at which Jenneca piloted it was far beyond the recommended safety limits.

"Shouldn't I be driving?" Trainer yelled over the roar of the wind above their heads.

"No you should not," Jenneca replied.

"You realize this is highly irregular."

"I am aware. Sometimes irregular is good."

"I've been instructing royals in the same manner for generations. It hasn't failed me yet."

"Sure, but don't you ever get tired of the people you train resenting you?"

"No one resents me."

"They do a little bit."

"They always come out thankful for my expertise and instruction."

"Sometimes, but wouldn't you rather they not resent you up until then?"

"Do you resent me?"

"I refuse to answer that on the grounds that I don't have to."

"And why did you bring the servant girl?"

"Her name's Naoke. She's a royal attendant."

"I know her station."

"She's here in case we need anything."

"I've brought lemonade," Naoke announced from the back where she was seated beside Neva. A large opaque jug sat in her lap.

"Wonderful." Trainer braced himself against the dashboard. "And where are we going that a royal attendant would be of need?"

Shortly, Jenneca sat herself at the controls of another vehicle. This one was entirely enclosed, illuminated only by a few sparse running lights and the glow from the panel readouts of the forward and side consoles.

A uniformed soldier sat off to her right while Neva and Naoke occupied a pair of jump seats near the rear.

"General Bly, how'm I looking?" Jenneca asked into her headset.

Neva spoke up. "This feels like…"

"This feels like winning, is what this feels like," said Jenneca.

"I… question your definition of 'winning,'" said Neva

"General Bly, I repeat, how am I looking?"

"He's not answering," said Neva.

"I know he's not answering, which can't mean anything good."

The environment around them rumbled, throwing Neva off-balance in her seat and only further heightening her anxiety.

"This whole thing is a bad idea," she said. Her fingers reddened as they gripped tighter to the sides of her seat.

"Just stay focused," Jenneca instructed.

"Focused on what? What am I supposed to be learning from this?"

"Then you should be paying closer attention. Naoke gets it, right Naoke?"

"I spilled the lemonade, so I'm not sure what function I serve here."

"You can make more," said Jenneca. "Alright, everyone hang on. This is going to get bumpy."

"Going to get?" Neva asked.

Jenneca shoved forward on the shifters.

The vehicle lurched awkwardly, throttling along a rocky pass.

Its outsized treads tore along the dry, dusty terrain, towards a small ravine. By the time they had cleared it, they were already under fire from several opposing vehicles of similar design and armament.

"Return fire! Return fire!" Jenneca ordered.

"On it." The uniformed officer clutched the gun controls and opened up. Barrels blazed as they hurtled along.

"This is just a distraction!" Jenneca shouted over the rumble of the cabin. "Ready the grappling beams!"

"Ready." The gunner nodded, never taking her eyes off the targeting system before her. "On your command, princess."

Jenneca hissed through gritted teeth, "Annnnnd... now!"

A pair of long, clawed metallic lines launched from the front of the tank, snatching up a large swath of fabric held to a pole that was supported by a bundle of sandbags.

"Yes!" Jenneca whooped. "Consider that flag captured!"

"Is it over?" Neva asked.

"Is it over? Have you never played this before?"

"I've never played any games with tanks before."

"It's not... ugh, it's not just about capturing the flag. We have to make it back to our base with it."

"So now that we have it…"

"We are an even bigger target, yes."

A herd of tanks followed theirs, with more joining the pursuit as they sped along.

"They're swarming," said the gunner.

Jenneca smiled.

"Yeah they are."

The tank began to rock as plasma fire from their pursuers exploded all around.

"Can't we go any faster?" Neva asked.

"Not without the flag tearing loose," said Jenneca. "Trust me, this isn't my first go-around."

"What kind of stupid game is this then?" Neva asked.

Their tank bolted along, only just managing to remain ahead of their opponents.

A row of explosions set off in front of the enemy swarm, breaking their formation.

Another row of tanks, bearing the same colors as Jenneca's, zoomed past and engaged the scattering adversaries.

Trainer stood with General Bly, a fellow worn old vet, near a stack of rocks that held Jenneca's own flag. They watched as her tank skidded up and screeched to a halt.

The hatch atop it opened and Jenneca popped out about up to her waist.

"Yes! The winner and still the champion!"

"Very good, princess," said the general.

Jenneca climbed out and down the side of the tank. Neva followed close behind.

"And you're sure they didn't let you win because you're the princess?" she asked.

"No," said Bly. "Heavens no. Any officer would blush at the very idea."

"I'm just good at tank-capture-the-flag," said Jenneca.

"The troops do love it when you come to visit and bring your... unique sense of war games," Bly said.

"I suppose it's nice that someone enjoys it," said Trainer.

"Everyone enjoys it but you," Jenneca pointed out. "And that's probably just because you never play."

"It would be unfair. I taught these soldiers everything they know about tactics."

"The greatest gift a student can give a teacher is to surpass them."

"Says who?" asked Trainer.

"You'll never know if you've been surpassed if you refuse to give anyone an opportunity to prove themselves," said Jenneca.

More tanks rolled up to join them, sporting both sets of colors. One of the enemy tanks opened. A young man leaned out.

"Excellent job, princess. Shall we go again?"

Jenneca checked her timepiece.

"You know what? I think we shall." She climbed back up to her tank. "Come along, Neva."

CHAPTER 5

rainer still looked perturbed when the party returned to the castle.

"Well, it's just about the end of Neva's scheduled training," said Jenneca. "I'd call that a productive day."

"Not the word I'd use for it," said Trainer.

"That's because you're a grump."

The group carried along down the hallway back from the garage.

"I'm still cleaning lemonade out of my gown," Neva said. "I can be with you in a few moments."

"Eh, take the rest of the day off," said Jenneca.

Naoke curtsied.

"Thank you, princess."

She left them and made her way to an adjacent hall.

Catherine and Jason approached from further up the corridor.

"Hello Jenneca," said Catherine. "Hello Neva."

"Hello, Grand'ma," said Neva.

"How's the training going?" Catherine asked her.

"I… wish I knew."

"It went great," Jenneca said. "We took a little excursion."

"Oh, I wish I'd known you were going out," said Catherine.

"Why?" asked Jason.

"I'd like to go for a nice drive. It's been awhile."

"It wasn't a nice drive," said Jenneca. "We went to a

munitions testing range."

"Oh, of course. She just became a royal, why wouldn't the first thing she wants to see be our luxurious munitions testing ranges?"

"Grand'ma."

"I'm just teasing, honey. Though it wouldn't kill you to show her some of the finer parts of being a royal."

"It might, you don't know."

Catherine kissed her on the forehead.

"Try to stay optimistic. Look at the glass as half full."

"But full of what, though?" Jenneca asked.

"Don't be crude."

"I, uh, think I'm going to go be alone for a while," said Neva.

"Oh," said Jenneca. "Okay."

Neva headed away from the group.

"Did I say something to upset her?" Catherine asked.

Jenneca shrugged.

"I don't know."

"Did you?" asked Catherine

Jenneca groused to herself.

Neva stood on a line painted on the stone floor. About twenty meters up the alleyway was a target, about a meter wide, plastered against a porous wall.

In her left hand was a bow and in her right, an arrow. She nocked the arrow and drew back, taking time to carefully line up her shot before loosing. The arrow plunged into the outer ring of the target.

"Ech."

"You need to do that faster."

Neva jumped slightly at the sound of the queen's voice.

"Wha... I didn't even know you were here."

"I'm good at that. I can try teaching you someday, but,

maybe get the basics down first. Like archery."

"That's what I'm working on." She picked another arrow out of a nearby barrel.

"I know. You sneak off on your own often?"

"No. It's hard. I... I get nervous. I don't want people watching me, and it's hard to get in practice without Trainer knowing I'm here."

"Trainer knows you're here."

"No he doesn't."

"I wasn't asking. Now, about your form..."

"Look, I... can I just do this alone?" Neva asked.

"You can, if you don't want to get better fast. Listening to people who know what they're talking about is a good way to learn, though."

"Like I said, I get nervous. I don't do as good with people watching me."

"In combat, do you think your opponent won't be looking?"

"Combat?"

"Why do you think you're learning this? Members of the royal family are expected to fight for the empire. I mean, we still haven't quite worked out what your position is, but training won't hurt you either way."

"I broke two fingers sparring with Trainer earlier."

"You know, I knew it didn't sound right as soon as I said it. Look, I can leave you alone, but can I just point out some basics first?"

"I guess."

"Okay. You're taking too long to release. You have to be quicker. Nock, aim, loose. If you hold it, your drawing arm's going to get worn out real fast. You might do okay on the first few, but you're going to get sloppier and sloppier."

"But it takes me awhile to aim," Neva said.

"You aim with your eyes. Bringing the arrow into it is the last step. You only do that when you're ready to kill the thing you're looking at."

"But... okay, can I just show you?"

"Show me what?" Val asked.

"What I mean."

"Go ahead."

"Okay."

Neva raised the bow up, nocked the arrow, drew it back, slowly took aim, and fired it at the target. She made a decent, not great, hit.

"Okay, but when I do it your way..." She nocked the arrow, raised it, and fired. The arrow sailed askew and dug itself into the wall a good bit away from the target. "See?"

"Because you're not aiming before you fire."

"I'm trying, it just doesn't feel right."

"That's why you practice. Trust me. You just do it over and over again until the right way feels natural."

"Were you a natural at this?" Neva asked.

"Archery?"

"Yeah."

"I suppose. I mean... I don't know. I started doing it forever ago. I grew up a soldier. I trained on all kinds of weapons. I guess there was some natural ability there, but it also took a lot of hard work. A lot."

"Great." Neva held the bow down. "So it's just me then?"

"No. Look. I had two brothers. Prince Thoome and King Joseph. Thoome was probably more like me, but Joe definitely was not. He did not have a natural aptitude for physical activities like this, or sword fighting, or anything athletic."

"And did he ever get good at it?"

"He, uh, never got the chance. He died a couple days into his training."

"Oh." Neva's eyes darted away. "I'm... I'm sorry."

"You really don't follow opera, do you?" Val asked.

"I don't hate it, I just can't remember all of that."

"That is the history of our family, and our people. Okay, know what, I'm getting worked up here. I'm sorry. If you decide you want to try more opera, we have a box at the theater. If not, maybe I can learn about what you're into."

"Into?"

"Your interests," Val said. "Your hobbies. We're going to be spending an awful lot of time together. And you are my daughter, when it comes down to it. I'd like to know you."

"Oh. Okay. Yeah, sure."

"Did I phrase it weird? Is 'into' not something kids say anymore? Oh, God, am I getting that old?"

Neva shrugged.

"I am, aren't I?" Val asked. "To some degree I knew it. I'm not a teenager anymore. I have teenagers. Oof. Well, this has been eye-opening. I'll leave you alone now. But if you ever need any help or have any questions, I'm always around."

"Thanks."

Val smiled.

"Sure."

She left.

Neva picked up another arrow. She quickly nocked and loosed it. It came closer to the target than her previous attempt but still missed its mark by a fair margin.

She growled to herself.

Val reappeared behind her.

"What about school?" the queen asked.

Neva forcefully set the bow and arrows down and started to walk away.

"Whoa. Hey. Okay, I get it. School is a line."

"It's not just that," Neva said.

"Then what is it?"

Neva stood planted in place, stewing.

"Come on. I'm your..."

"My mother?" Neva asked.

"Sort of."

"But you're..." Neva growled. "And school's just another thing I can't do normal anymore."

"No, you can do it better than normal. You have royal tutors..."

"None of my friends will be there."

"You can still see your friends."

"What?"

"You're not a prisoner here. You're allowed guests. I'd hope you'd maybe want to get to know your siblings a bit, but if you want to invite friends over, just talk to any concierge."

Neva pulled back her hair.

"They're the guys with the hats," said Val. "Really you can talk to just about anyone, if they can't make something happen, they'll point you toward who can."

"Okay."

Neva moved past the neglected bow as she marched away from her biological mother.

Naoke looked down at her dress as she walked along, holding it outward so to get a good look at the stain down the front of it.

With no one else around, she peeled it off – leaving her in her slip – and made a quick turn into the throne room.

Upon entering, she walked to the symbol in the center of the floor and paced around it. The pillar rose up from its surface. The Crown of the Ten Point Star rested atop there.

Naoke lifted it and stared at it for a moment, glaring at it with a mix of admiration and disdain.

She turned to leave only to find Val standing in the doorway.

"Naoke, what are you doing?"

Naoke held her hands up. The Crown dangled from one of her fingertips.

"Oops."

"Answer me."

Naoke looked at the Crown.

"No, I don't think I will."

"This looks bad for you," said Val.

"Does it?"

"Put the Crown down and answer me."

Naoke chuckled.

"'Crown down.' That rhymes."

"Guards!"

A group of armed palace guards rushed into the room, weapons at the ready.

Val pointed at Naoke.

"Seize her."

The soldiers grabbed Naoke and forced her hands behind her back. Val plucked the Crown from her grasp and stood aside as she was put in manacles and led away.

CHAPTER 6

A magistrate paced the front of the small courtroom. Near to him was a defendant's table, to which Naoke was shackled. No one else was present.

"By law, you'll be charged with sedition, the punishment for which is execution," he explained to her. "If you'd like, you have the option of a private execution, attended only by the royalty and..."

"You'll never make this stick."

"We, I... what? You were caught with the Crown of the Ten Point Star on your person."

"Uh-huh," she said. "The execution may be private, what about the trial?"

"That is up to the queen."

"I demand a public trial."

"That isn't how this works."

"No, we'll definitely be granting that." Val entered, along with her usual retinue of attendants, soldiers, and her guardian.

Naoke looked at her, a slight smirk curling onto her lips.

"I want to know why," Val said, "and if the whole kingdom hears it at the same time, that's fine by me."

"I'm not sure you'll like the answer," said Naoke.

"Don't worry about what I like. Has anyone here ever mistreated you? Have we not made you feel welcome? You've been here a year and you betray me now? I don't understand."

"No, you wouldn't, would you? Because the Ten Point

crown doesn't work the same as the Five Point, does it?"

"And what's that supposed to mean?"

"One of the benefits of the Five Point crown is granting its bearer great wisdom and insight," Naoke said. "You couldn't even see what was happening in your own home all these years."

"That's not what that means."

"Trust me, it does."

"No, it... what would you know about it?"

"Isn't it obvious by now?" Naoke asked.

"Isn't what obvious?"

The younger girl burst out laughing.

"You really have no idea, do you?"

"Enough of this vaguery," Val snapped. "Speak straight and plain, or you'll be held in contempt."

"I'm sorry," Naoke said. "You'd be right that I should show more deference to your position."

"If that's what you need to tell yourself."

"But we all know you're not the legitimate inheritor of that position."

Val's head dropped.

"Oh. So you're one of those people."

Naoke smiled.

"You've no idea who I am. And I find that hilarious."

"You're going to tell me..."

"I am. And I'll make you show deference to the position."

"You have no position," Val said. "You are not a member of the royal family."

Naoke laughed.

"But I am. That's what's so grand about this. I am the rightful Queen of Kaia."

"So you're just insane."

"No. I'm the heir of the once and true ruler of the empire."

"Care to show me where you appear in the operas?" Val asked.

"I don't need a fancy song to know my place. I am the true scion of this world and its holdings and have been since my birth."

"Okay," Val said. "We're done here."

"Oh, not even close. We're just getting started, you and I."

"Sure."

"It'll end when I've launched you and your substandard crown into the sun. Just like you did to my father."

The color drained from Val's face.

"What? What did you say?"

"That got your attention."

Val snarled at her. "Prove it. Give me one reason to think you're Angelo's daughter."

"I don't have to answer to you, cousin."

"Angelo had no heirs! He spent his life in service..."

"To my uncle, Andor. It was only in the last months of his life that he took a wife. Or, wives. My mothers. Kavana and Clerak."

"That's all been recorded. Everyone knows their names."

"Maybe. Does everyone know that you let Kavana flee when you confronted Angelo on Earth?"

Val straightened up.

"They don't, do they?" Naoke asked. "Little did you know I was already growing in her belly. Fewer people knew of that than knew that my father kept your mother alive by artificial means."

The hardened lines of Val's scowl deepened.

"We have ways of verifying..."

"Please do."

"If any hint of this turns out to be true, how do you see this ending?"

"I see it ending with one of us dead," Naoke said. "And it won't be me."

Val backed away from the table. The magistrate stood froze, off to one side of the room.

"Oh, and cousin," the girl at the table said. "You may address me by my true name from now on. No need for pretense. I'm called Angela."

BOOK 4: OF THE CENTURY

CHAPTER 1

Val sat alone in the throne room: slouched, her hands clasped before her, her elbows braced on the plush armrests.

She wasn't in the habit of spending much time in the chamber nor sat on the ceremonial seat, yet there she was.

From her perch on the stone dais against the far wall, her gaze was lost somewhere beyond the crown that sat perched on the pedestal in the room's center.

Bontu entered; the light spilling in from the hallway broke the dismal mood that the queen had cultivated.

"The results have come back," he said.

The hands in front of her face came down.

"I don't think I need the wisdom of the Crown to know what they say."

"They confirm it." He held out a data pad towards her. "She's Angelo and Kavana's daughter, and your cousin. It's a girl."

"You know, I've tried over the years to have Kavana found," Val said. "Clerak, too, if she was still alive. One thing they were always better at than us is sorcery."

"Trickery, too, I suppose."

"Using the magic for the trickery," she said. "How did a spoiled little brat like Kavana ever become so adept at the mystic arts when we can barely keep up our mages' ranks?"

"The same way I stayed alive so many years on that ice world. Necessity."

"This is a bad situation."

"You've survived worse."

"No I haven't. Nothing like this. Even when I took the Crown, Angelo was dead. Now his living, breathing heir turns up... this could destroy the crown."

"No. Nothing can destroy the Crown, short of launching it into a sun."

Val glared at him.

"Oh, you mean... uh, well then yes, this could be disastrous."

"How are the barristers coming with the case?" Val asked.

"They say they're doing well. Forgive my simplicity, but this seems like a fairly easy decision. You have the Crown. You're the queen. You've sat on the throne for near twenty years. She has no claim..."

"She's Angelo's daughter, and he held the throne before me. There's long been a preference for a contiguous line of succession."

"And you're Andor's daughter. So, the line goes from him to you."

Val shook her head.

"If it had, this would be a lot simpler. But it went from Andor, to Joe, to Angelo, to me. And there was a civil war in there, don't forget."

"I'm not forgetting that."

"The laws of succession can be somewhat tortuous," she said. "I've never understood why some of the clauses in them were enacted, but here we are."

"Would you like me to look into it?"

Val cocked an eyebrow at him. "I don't know what to do. So I'm doing what I said I would. I said we'd give her a public trial, so we will. And I swore to always be truthful with the people of Kaia, so I will."

"Didn't you also swear to defeat or destroy any enemies of the crown?"

"I did. I'd rather that not include family members, if at all possible."

    "What if she doesn't give you a choice?" he asked.

    "That's very much a 'cross that bridge when you come to it' kind of scenario."

CHAPTER 2

Val's children had gathered nearby a doorway into the courtroom. Neva was included, though her manner of dress was not as elaborate as the others. She knew she was required to wear a skirt or dress, per custom, but hadn't yet had the time to develop the taste for the fineries that her newly discovered siblings had.

Though none would admit it, the children all shook with a nervous energy as they awaited the approach of their mother.

And approach she did, dressed not only in an elaborate scarlet gown and the Crown on her forehead, but with a heavy cloak slung around her shoulders. It dragged the ground behind her, so much so that Bontu had to remain off to one side as he accompanied her to where her children stood.

"You know, none of you are under any obligation to be here," she told them.

"If you are..." said Jenneca.

"I'm here because I'm the queen. But if you don't feel comfortable at all sitting through this, no one will think any less of you."

The children were quiet.

"Can we just get on with it?" Jenneca asked.

Val gave a tepid smile.

The main feature of the castle's Wing of Justice was the grand courtroom. The walls were adorned with a series of columns interspersed with statues dedicated to the Kaian depictions of justice: women holding swords, men carrying bundles of sticks, children lofting baskets.

On one side of the courtroom was the magistrate's bench; the main entrance was opposite it, a pair of heavy wooden doors with hinges and hangers as old as any structure in Olivert. The viewing gallery had two levels, easily capable of holding more than a thousand spectators. There were even more standing in the corridor outside, trying to peer in. As the trial was public, the doors had been left open, and holos of the proceedings were projected around the building.

There were two sets of doors on either side of the magistrate's bench. To the left was the pathway to the holding cells, where the accused was moved in and out. To the right, the chambers for the royals and their representatives.

The right-hand doors opened and Val and her children filed in. The assembled crowd rose to their feet as the royal family made their way to the first row of floor gallery seating.

The crowd sat as soon as Val did. She was stoic and regal, never once acknowledging the throngs of onlookers.

Bontu was seated next to Val, on her right. Jenneca and Neva sat on the other side of him, while Joseph and Sanke were to Val's left.

An armed bailiff, one of several stationed throughout the room, moved to the front of the magistrate's bench.

"All rise for the honorable magistrate!"

The court again stood, even the royals.

The magistrate entered through a small door behind his bench. He set down a pad and sat.

He was an older man, bedecked in a bright blue robe with intricate gold and silver stitching running around the cuffs and up the sleeves.

He nodded to the bailiff.

"Bring in the prisoner," said the bailiff.

The other set of doors opened. Angela, in manacles, was led to a table nearby the witness stand. Several barristers of her own sat with her. They scowled to themselves and, after briefly glancing towards their charge, each stared straight ahead.

The nearby jury box sat empty.

A barrister entered from the royals' door. Much younger than the magistrate, he nevertheless wore similarly opulent robes.

He walked to the front of the hall and looked around for a moment before turning to Angela.

"The prosecution calls the accused to the stand for first examination."

Angela stood and confidently walked to the witness stand, where she seated herself, never once allowing the chains that bound her to hinder the gracefulness of her movement.

"I have been selected to represent the interests of the crown. That's crown with a lowercase 'C,' despite the argument at the basis of this case. Attendant Naoke, you stand accused of attempted theft of the Crown with a capital 'C.' How do you plead? You may confer with your representatives, if you so choose."

"I cannot answer," she said.

"You must enter a plea for the trial to proceed."

"I reject the basis of the accusation. I stand accused of theft of property that is rightfully mine."

"The Crown is the property of the monarchy. It currently belongs to our beloved queen, Valentina."

"Here it comes," Val muttered to herself.

"It is, by rights, mine. I am Angela, daughter of King Angelo and Queen Kavana of Kaia and the true heir to the Crown."

Save the queen's retinue and her barristers, the courtroom rang out in a wave of audible gasps and grumblings.

The magistrate slammed his ceremonial stone on the desk plate.

"Order. Order in the court, or we'll have the observation

deck cleared."

"I was promised a public trial," Angela said.

"And so you'll have, so long as the court has order."

The crowd settled down even as reporters tapped away at their communication devices.

The barrister approached the magistrate.

"Your honor, though this news comes as a shock to most in the courtroom today, the queen has been made previously aware of this assertion and is willing to attest to its validity."

The magistrate looked to Val.

"For the record, this is the truth, your highness?"

Val stood.

"It is, your honor. Genetic tests were run on the girl at my request. They verified her claims. The girl who called herself Naoke is my first cousin by my Uncle Angelo."

The courtroom grumbled again.

The magistrate raised his stone. A hush fell over the room.

"I made a vow to always be truthful with the people of Kaia," Val said, "and this is the truth, to the best of my knowledge."

"Thank you, your highness," said the magistrate.

Val nodded and sat back down.

The magistrate looked to the barrister.

"You may continue, counselor."

"Thank you, your honor." He moved towards the witness stand again. "Angela... or is it Naoke? Which do you prefer?"

"Who gives a damn what she prefers?" Val whispered.

Bontu leaned towards her. "Propriety."

"Propriety can shove it."

"Oh, I heartily agree."

"Angela," the girl on the witness stand said. "That's the name my mothers gave me."

"Very well," said the barrister. "Angela. You entered the castle under false pretenses, disguised as an attendant named Naoke. Why should anyone trust a thing you say?"

"I entered the castle the way I did because I feared for my

life if I was discovered."

"If you were discovered? Why risk coming to the castle at all?"

"I meant if my existence was discovered by the queen. She's had agents hunting for my mothers all my life. She killed my father to obtain her title. I'd no reason to believe she wouldn't see me as a threat."

Val shrugged. "I mean, there were circumstances."

"That's why I wanted this trial to be public," Angela continued. "To ensure my safety as much as is possible under Valentina's eye."

"To be clear," said the barrister, "has Queen Valentina ever made any threats, explicitly or implicitly towards you?"

"She's not had the chance."

"I'll take that as a no."

"Sure," muttered Val, "now ask if she's threatened me."

"I turned myself in before she knew who I was," Angela stated.

"You turned yourself in?" the barrister asked. "Records show you were caught in the act of stealing the Crown of the Ten Point Star."

"I'd no illusions of making it out of the castle with the Crown."

"Then why make the attempt?"

"To garner the queen's attention."

The barrister plucked a pad off his table and slowly scrolled through its text.

"Witnesses have heard the queen refer to you by name, as she does with much of the palace staff. She already seemed to know you. Earlier on the day you were arrested, you'd gone with Princesses Jenneca and Neva on an excursion."

"Where they humiliated me for their fun," said Angela.

"Humiliated you how?" the barrister asked.

"Poured lemonade over me and forced me to sit in it for hours. I was finally on my way to clean myself when the opportunity to make myself known to the queen was presented to me."

Val looked around Bontu to shoot a glance towards Jenneca and Neva.

"She's lying," said Jenneca.

Seemingly satisfied with that answer, Val leaned back and returned her attention to the testimony at hand.

"And that was when you saw your opening to attempt to steal the Crown?" the barrister asked.

"Again I reject the premise of the questioning. By rights, that crown is mine, as is the palace and the whole of the Kaian Star Empire."

"You are not sat on the throne," the barrister said. "You've received no coronation."

"A ceremony doesn't decide who rightfully rules Kaia."

"No, but the laws of succession do."

"My father was a legitimately sat king…"

"Your father murdered his own family to attain his position."

"And my cousin murdered him to take it for herself. Do two wrongs make a right?"

"We're not here to argue that."

"Aren't we? The entire case against me rests on the notion that I am not the legitimate ruler. If I'm correct, then this trial is, at the very best, unnecessary."

"Ugh," said Val. "Why couldn't she just challenge me to combat and we could have it over with?"

"Because you'd destroy her and she knows it," said Bontu.

"Yeah, but it'd be so much easier on everyone."

"Except her."

"Eh. The needs of the many and all that."

"What?"

"Beg pardon?"

"The needs of the many what?" Bontu asked.

"The needs of the many outweigh the needs of the few," said Val. "Have you seriously never heard that before? It's not an uncommon saying."

"I must've missed that growing up."

"Miss, ah, Angela, you're aware that theft of the Crown is a capital offense?" asked the barrister.

"I am."

"Just because you were unsuccessful doesn't negate the severity of what you did. If you wish for any leniency, cooperation would be a healthy way to start asking for it."

"Were you aware that assault of a royal is also a capital offense?" asked Angela.

"Uh, I don't see what that has to..."

Angela looked directly at Val.

"The queen can grant leniency at her leisure."

Val's face flushed. Her brow furrowed.

The barrister looked back at Val.

"Yes, well, that is neither here nor there," the barrister said. "You're here today to answer for the crime of theft of the Crown. Do you admit that you entered the throne room without permission?"

"One needn't ask permission to move freely in one's own home."

"Did you receive authorization from the queen or any member of the royal family to be in that room?"

"I am a member of the royal family."

Bontu leaned in towards Val.

"Well, she's not actually wrong about that."

"And a broken clock is right twice a day."

"I've never heard that expression before, either."

"Even amongst members of the royal family, the Crown is off-limits to all but the current bearer," said the barrister. "Did you take the Crown from its display case without permission from the queen? Will you at least confirm that fact?"

"I am the queen," said Angela.

"Ms. Angela, might I remind you that you have representatives today in the court. Do you wish to confer with any of them before answering these questions?"

"No."

"So be it. You, Angela, daughter of Angelo, are not the queen."

"My father was the rightful king..."

"His reign was short and ended more than seventeen years ago. Valentina is the rightful queen. You are charged with theft involving an act of sedition. How do you plead?"

"I cannot be guilty of anything you accuse me of because I am the queen."

"Young lady, if you're looking for an insanity defense, I doubt you'll have much luck."

Angela's voice raised but physically she was unmoved.

"I am not insane! I'm the bloody queen!"

CHAPTER 3

Back in the royal chambers, Val and the barrister stood around the table at the windowless room's center, on which was piled the barrister's notepads.

"So, how do we think we're doing?" she asked.

"Apart from her bringing up Prince... ah, I mean, your son. Um... I'm sorry, your highness."

"It's... just answer the question, please."

"Aside from that, I would say we seem to be doing well, your highness. Perhaps a bit too well."

"How can we be doing too well?"

"The defendant is barely defending herself. She's offering no real exonerating evidence or testimony."

"Because there isn't any. She was caught red-handed."

"And choosing to represent herself seems... foolish."

"To put it kindly."

The barrister took a breath.

"I'm not sure what else to say, my queen. Her behavior is strange, her assertions... well, the crowd was already reeling from the revelation of her identity, but I doubt her assertions will garner her any public favor."

"We don't need to worry about the public. This isn't a jury trial. How do you think this is all playing with the magistrate?"

"Not well, I'd suppose. He hates outbursts and is rarely favorable to grand displays of emotion."

"And what do you think she's playing at?"

"My queen?"

"Like you said, she's doing a pretty poor job defending herself. I wouldn't put money on her being flat out incompetent."

"No, my queen. I... if you're worried I'll underestimate her..."

"No. No, that's not what I'm worried about. I'm worried she has some kind of hidden plan or something that we're just not seeing."

"She does keep changing the subject, bringing up her supposed claim to the throne rather than answering for the theft."

"Yeah. I don't know if she really believes it, or... I don't know, or this is all part of her game."

"The entire point of these sorts of trials is to ferret out the truth. I've no doubt it will be the same here."

Val gave him a smile.

"I have every confidence in you to do that."

They returned to the courtroom shortly thereafter.

"Hear ye, court is again in session," the bailiff announced. "His honor presides."

"Thank you." The magistrate nodded. "Counselor."

The barrister approached the witness stand, where Angela again sat.

"I would like to begin this session by again asking the defendant how she pleads to the charge of theft of the Crown."

Angela glared at him.

One of her representatives stood.

"Your honor, I would ask that this line of questioning be brought to a halt, for all our sakes. It is clear that my client is unwilling to answer the prosecutor's questions as asked."

The magistrate sighed.

"Your client has agreed to testify, and so she shall until the prosecutor ends his examination. Furthermore, she has waived her right to counsel, so while you'll not be discharged from the court, you are not entitled to speak on her behalf."

The representative frowned as he took his chair.

"However," said the magistrate, "as the accused has not answered to the basic charge of the matter, the court will enter a plea of 'not guilty' on her behalf so as to allow the proceedings to begin in earnest."

"Thank you, your honor," said the barrister. He turned his attention to Angela. "So, Ms. Angela, now that we've a plea of not guilty entered on your account, I would like to ask what your intentions were on the day in question."

"I believe I've already answered to that."

"You touched upon it, briefly, but the court wants to be as thorough as possible. Let us never say you were not given an adequate chance to defend yourself."

"How kind of you. It's positively Celleavian."

"Beg pardon?" the barrister asked.

"Oh," Val's voice popped. "Crap. Oh, no."

She waved to her barrister, who turned to the magistrate.

"Ah, your honor, may we move for a recess?"

"Another?" the magistrate asked.

"Yes, your honor. I apologize, but something has just, ah, entered the prosecution's mind."

"Very well. We'll take a ten-minute recess." He slammed his ceremonial stone on the desk.

"The court is now in recess," said the bailiff.

The barrister rushed over to Val.

"What is it, my queen?"

"King Sigworth."

"My queen?"

"King Sigworth, who fought the battle of Celleavia, took the throne... oh crap. His uncle, Para, had been the king, but instead of passing the Crown to any of Para's children, it passed to Sigworth."

"Why?"

"Because Sigworth's father, Easam, took the throne when Para fell ill and none of Para's children were found to be fit."

"So you're saying…"

"I'm saying, there's precedent for the case she's trying to make." Val barely glanced at Angela but that was more than enough to confirm that the younger girl was staring at her.

"A portion of it, at least," said the barrister. "But that's one instance, hardly…"

"One instance that led to the current lineage. The royal bloodline has more than a few irregularities in it. I don't think anyone's ever tried to get a court ruling on one before."

"Nor do I believe she'll get one now."

"I don't either, but she could be planning to sow doubt with her testimony."

"I understand, my queen. I'll not let her."

"Thank you. I'll hold you to that."

"Court is again in session."

"Thank you," said the barrister. "Ms. Angela, I would ask that you answer the previous question before continuing. I can repeat it, if you need."

"No, thank you. I have an excellent memory. Long and deep."

"That's fine to hear. And your answer?"

"My goal upon entering the throne room was to wrest the Crown from its holding spot."

"And your plans after that?"

"Who's to say I had any?"

"If your memory is long and deep, I have no reason to believe your foresight is not equally adept."

"That's very kind of you."

"And your answer, Ms. Angela?"

"Best case scenario, I'd make it back to my room with the Crown and decide what to do from there. As I'd said before, I'd no illusions of making it out of the castle with the Crown, nor any strong desire to."

"Why not?" the barrister asked.

"Beg pardon?"

"Why not try to make it out of the castle?"

"Do you think I could have?"

"I think you're a clever woman. Surely someone who was clever enough to infiltrate the castle would be clever enough to work out a scenario to extricate herself."

"Not with the Crown."

"I'd think the Crown would make it easier. You're of the blood, as the queen has testified to. Could you not have simply donned the Crown and forced your way out, even once discovered?"

"Perhaps you're cleverer than I."

"But why not do that, is the question we keep circling round to."

"Because that wasn't my goal. Isn't my goal. I desire that which is mine by right, the throne of Kaia. Absconding with a pilfered artifact wouldn't bring that to me. Besides, Valentina has demonstrated in her lifetime a remarkable propensity for locating the Crowns. I've waited sixteen-odd years for my opportunity to take my birthright. I've no patience for allowing my cousin to muck about in any plans I might have."

"So you planned to be arrested?" he asked.

"Yes."

"And you planned to end up on trial, confessing now."

"I've confessed to nothing."

"Testifying then."

"Yes."

"To what end?"

"To let the people know the truth."

"And what truth is that?"

"That King Angelo's heir is out there. Here, now. That there is a better way than the path that the false queen has led them down for longer than I've been alive."

"I'm not going to engage with you regarding the queen's record."

Angela turned to the magistrate.

"Then you, your honor. Will you admit my case has more than merit?"

"My role here is to sit as an impartial judge," he told her.

"You may rule as to what testimony is and is not allowed, though. Isn't that correct?"

"Yes, but I cannot order the queen's barrister to ask specific questions."

"Nor may he be allowed to bar specific testimony without your approval."

"Young lady, I know fully well what my role in this courtroom is. I do not require any instruction."

Angela grumbled as she sat back.

"Very well. I'll sit on the matter until allowed to cross-examine."

"That is certainly your right," said the barrister. "I would remind you again that the queen you're so eager to besmirch is allowing you your full rights and privileges as the accused."

"I shouldn't be accused at all."

"I'm not engaging on that point, either. You stand accused of theft, and that is the crime for which I intend to prosecute."

"Did you not also say earlier that I stand accused of sedition?"

"The theft is the sedition. I will not be goaded into an argument over whether you are the queen of Kaia. You are not."

"Are you done with your examination yet? I have things I'd like to say on my behalf."

The barrister looked to Val. She nudged an eyebrow upward.

"Very well," he said. "The prosecution reserves the right to redirect."

"Thank you." Angela held out her wrists. "May I?"

The magistrate shook his head.

"The defendant was ordered manacled for a reason."

"I'll be able to mount a better defense if I were not so encumbered."

"You'll have to make do as-is," said the magistrate.

"Very well." Angela threw herself to her feet. The bailiffs moved towards her, their hands on their weapons. "I am shackled to a degree that I cannot relieve myself without assistance. I am not a danger, gentlemen."

The bailiffs waited for a look from the magistrate before backing off and returned to their assigned posts.

Angela began pacing in the witness box, which didn't get her very far in any direction.

"I stand here today accused of theft from the monarchy, a crime for which the punishment is potentially death. I have already belabored the point that I am a member of the monarchy in a very real sense, a fact to which the so-called queen has already attested. My prosecutor has made mention that the Crown itself is off-limits to all royals except the king or queen to whom it belongs." Angela smiled at Val. "I'll not make mention of how loosely the so-called queen enforces such rules amongst the royal family on a regular basis. No, instead I'll dive straight to the heart of the matter. To whom does the Crown truly belong? That is the center of this trial, whether the prosecution wishes to acknowledge it or not. One cannot steal from oneself. One cannot commit sedition if one is themselves the queen."

"Your honor," the barrister huffed, "the prosecution will gladly agree to the defense's most recent pair of assertions. But the defense has yet to offer any degree of evidence that she is, in fact, a rightful scion. Just saying it is so does not make it thus."

"If I may be allowed to continue?" Angela asked.

"You may," said the magistrate, "but keep in mind that in introducing such assertions about your standing, the burden of proof is on you."

"Understood. Yes, my status as a relative of the sitting queen is not in dispute. It's rather the matter of succession."

"Your honor, it is not the place of the court to settle matters of succession," the barrister said, his weary voice carrying a heaviness to it.

"Oh, but it is," Angela said. "In times when the order of succession is in dispute, it falls to the Council of Justice to determine rightful ascendency. The magistrate is a duly appointed representative of the Minister of Justice, though if the prosecution requires, I can request the minister herself attend to the matter."

"Your honor, the order of succession is not in dispute," said the barrister.

"I'm disputing it," said Angela.

"You have no legal standing..."

"Being the offspring of a former king gives me that right."

"I have to agree with the defense on this matter," said the magistrate. "She is allowed to bring disputes to succession before members of the judiciary."

Angela smiled at Val, a gesture which was not returned.

"The populace prefers a straight line of succession whenever possible," said Angela. "However, in Kaia's history, there have been multiple instances where that simply hasn't been possible. I'm sure even Valentina can call to mind some examples. When the trunk of the family tree became knotted and gnarled. When certain kings or queens were unable to pass the Crown straight downward."

Val stood.

"Your honor, if the defendant is going to challenge the validity of my claim to the throne, that changes the nature of this trial entirely."

"It would seem to, yes," said the magistrate.

"I'll agree," added Angela.

"Given that this is the turn things have taken," said Val, "I would ask for a recess, yes, another one, to confer with the legal team representing my interests."

"Oh, I've no objections to that at all," said Angela.

"Very well." The magistrate banged his ceremonial stone. "The court will reconvene in two hours' time."

"The court is now in recess," announced the bailiff.

"Does he have to do that every time?" Val asked.

"I believe that's literally part of his job," said Bontu.

CHAPTER 4

Val's children streamed out into the hallway outside their barrister's chambers.

"Well," Jenneca said, "look at it this way: we may not have to worry about figuring out who gets the Crown."

"That's not funny," said Sanke.

"And what do you want me to do?" Jenneca asked. "Just sit around moping?"

"That'd be more appropriate."

"And I've already done plenty of it. Look, mom's going to figure this out. There's no way she lets Naoke... er, Angela, take the throne. Absolutely none. There's not a lot we can do until then. We just have to keep showing up."

"How long is this trial going to last?" asked Joseph.

"It's barely a trial," said Jenneca.

"That doesn't answer the question."

"I don't know. It's not like there's a lot of evidence to enter. It's all just opinions and... I don't even know what."

Val again found herself in the royal barrister's chambers, sat at the central table with Bontu and the barrister.

"This is what I was talking about," Val said. "This is what I was worried about."

"We'll not let this child defeat us," said Bontu.

"No, we won't," the barrister agreed. "But, if she's going to be bringing ancient precedent into it... my queen, I'm a barrister, not an historian."

"I'm not technically either, but I know my opera."

"All due deference, my queen, but dramatic history isn't the same as case law."

Val sighed.

"What do you need from me?"

"I've several colleagues who'd be more qualified for the case as it's unfolded."

"I thought you were the best lawyer in the stable?" Bontu asked.

"I've the best record, and am probably the most knowledgeable when it comes to high crimes against the throne."

Val rose from the table.

"Bring in whoever you need to. And get it done fast. Say it's a special favor to the throne."

The barrister nodded.

"Yes, my queen."

Bontu started to get up.

"Should I...?"

"No," said Val.

Bontu was left behind as Val left.

He stared at the barrister, who hurriedly scrolled through the contacts in his comm device.

Bontu smiled warmly.

"So, how are you?"

Within the defense's chambers was a literal holding cell – iron bars and all – for keeping the most dangerous of defendants in place.

Angela sat in that barred-off section, with only a single guard in the room.

Val entered; she nodded to the guard, who picked up his reading pad and exited.

"Is this proper?" Angela asked from her perch on the small padded bench within.

"Do you care?"

Angela shrugged.

"Are you here to kill me then?"

"No. Despite what you're trying to get the courtroom and the public to believe, I have no plans of that."

"I'm not sure I believe that."

"It doesn't matter a great deal what the hell you believe."

"I think this court case is shaping up to prove that it does."

"You believe you're owed the throne. That'll never happen."

"That choice might not be yours. That's something you've never learned, it seems. Just because you're the queen doesn't mean you'll always get your way."

"I'm not too worried about that."

"Yes you are. If you weren't, you wouldn't be here right now."

"I'm..." Val took a pause to let out a sigh, "I'm here right now to try to reason with you."

"That won't work."

"I still have to hope..."

"No," said Angela, "it won't work because you simply can't see what's going on. You're not on my level, intellectually. You never even noticed? The pseudonym I chose for myself: Naoke?"

Val stared at her.

"It means 'the heart of the lion.' As is my father's title, the Lion of Kaia."

"I have never once heard him referred to that way." Val stepped closer. "Did your moms tell you that?"

Angela was silent.

"You're probably going to find out that a lot of what they've told you is bullshit," said Val. "About your father, about me, maybe even about yourself. This is a dangerous game you're playing."

"It's not a game."

"You're treating it like one. I've been trying to give you a way out. Give me a reason to keep trying."

"Now why would I want a way out? I've spent years of my life working my way in, and everything's going exactly to plan."

"No matter what happens, I don't think things are going to turn out the way you expect."

"Nor for you, cousin."

Val and her retinue reentered the courtroom and took their seats. A second barrister accompanied his colleague to the prosecution's table, this one an old, storied-looking fellow.

Angela was brought in.

"All rise."

The magistrate entered and was seated.

"You may be seated."

The magistrate looked to Angela.

"Young lady, you may proceed."

"Thank you, your honor. It's no secret that the lineage of the royal family has often been defined by the will of the people. The fact that Kaia still has a royal family was decided on by a popular vote generations ago, and the concept has been revisited since. Often. But more than that, the people decide who is fit to rule them. When Valentina took the throne from my father, there were protests against her reign."

The older barrister for the royals stood.

"Your honor, Barrister Ulcen Dorrster for the prosecution. The defendant is wildly misconstruing the nature by which succession is determined. As was well known, and proven by Queen Valentina's ascension, the internal workings of the royal family are largely private and intentionally mysterious."

"Is there an objection in there somewhere, or did you just wish to interrupt?" Angela asked.

"The objection is that the witness' testimony is dangerously close to perjury," Ulcen said.

"The prosecution will have a chance to redirect after the defense's examination," said the magistrate. "Proceed, Ms. Angela."

"Thank you again, your honor. Though, in light of recent revelations to the court about my heritage, it would be more appropriate that I be addressed, at the very least, as Lady Angela until such a time as my sovereignty is legally acknowledged."

Val's face dropped into her palm.

"Oh for... fine, your honor. As she is a member of the royal family, she may refer to herself by her royal title until such time as it is legally stripped from her," Val said.

"Very gracious of you, your highness," said the magistrate.

"We would like to add that she is not, however, recognized as a member of the royal family in good standing," said Val.

"Very well," said the magistrate. "You may again proceed, Lady Angela."

"As I said, historically, the royal family's existence and maintenance hinges largely on the will of the Kaian people. It was by their acceptance that my father was sat on the throne, but it was not ever truly accepted that Valentina was the legitimate queen. My father was beloved and celebrated in his time. Regardless of how he came to be monarch, there were no protests of his rule. Valentina never enjoyed the level of acceptance that my father did, despite similarly murdering her own family to take the throne. It is my thesis that she, who never bore the Crown of the Five Point Star that our ancestors long bowed to, is not a legitimate queen. It should be acknowledged that the descendant of the last true royal to wear that Crown is the rightful heir to the throne."

Ulcen rose up again.

"Your honor, if I may...?"

Angela tried to throw her arms wide but was blocked by the shackles that still held her wrists.

"I am through for the moment, your honor," she said.

Ulcen approached the bench.

"I believe the defense is, to put it politely, a bit naïve regarding her history. It's understandable, since she was not there to witness it. The civil war that led Valentina to the throne was, in fact, a contentious time for our people. Some did genuinely love Angelo, others were merely afraid. And with good reason. There were no protests because no one wanted to die. People died the day of his wedding. Despite any flaws she may have had or has as a ruler, there's no threat from Queen Valentina like that."

"There's no threat of violence on her wedding day because Valentina never married," said Angela. "An unmarried scion? She flouts tradition at every turn."

"She has been an exemplary ruler, only hindered by the upheaval your father purposefully inflicted on the kingdom. But we are not here to argue that."

"Aren't we?"

"No."

"We're here to argue the legitimacy of her reign. Her fitness for her station is at the center of that," said Angela.

"Regardless of what you may think, Queen Valentina is sat on the throne. It is incumbent upon the defense to prove there is any cause to remove her."

"The cause is that she never should have been there. Tell me, counselor, are you familiar with the code dictating the order of succession?"

"As someone who is not a member of the royal family, even I am not privy to all its secrets. Nor would you have been, living in exile for all your life."

"I am referring of course to the public records, tied to the upholding of the royal lineage. Section four, subsection sixteen, states that the member of the royal family who possesses the Crown of the Five Point Star shall be one and the same with the member who sits upon the throne and governs the people of Kaia. Do you acknowledge this?"

"I do. Though the Crown of the Five Point Star was lost

when your father died."

"Destroyed by my cousin Valentina, yes. Section fifteen of the record states the order by which the Crown is passed between royals. Do you acknowledge this?"

"Yes, but again..."

"The Crown is passed first to the firstborn child of the current wearer. I again point out for the court that my father was the last legitimate ruler of the kingdom to bear the Crown. Thus, by royal law, governance should pass to his first, and in this case only, heir, that being myself."

"Had Angelo died while sat on the throne, and had his reign been legitimate..."

"It was."

"Not according to the royal record."

"A record that was altered by Valentina after his reign. During his time on the throne there was no question as to his legitimacy."

"No question? Young lady, a war was fought over the question. Thousands of good soldiers died believing in the cause of removing him from the throne."

"And just as many died to keep him there."

"The prosecution will not deny that there was, among the populace, a percentage that supported Angelo," Ulcen said. "Many more were simply doing as they were ordered. Those that fought back all did so out of conviction, if the defense wishes to keep using the 'will of the people' as a cause for questioning someone's legitimacy."

"Are you suggesting that, if I wish to unseat Valentina, I should be prepared to go to war?"

Ulcen laughed.

"Ms. Angela, this war will be fought with words, on the battlefield of this courtroom. That is the war for which you should have prepared yourself."

"I did, and I have. Thank you, counselor, your testimony today has been most helpful. But I'm through with this now."

She stood. The bailiffs all moved towards her, their hands

again on the weapons holstered at their sides.

"My mothers have arrived and with them brought irrefutable proof of my sovereignty," she said.

"What?" asked Val.

A din built in the courtroom as the spectators at the rear doors parted.

Kavana, former princess of Palan, confidently strode in. Her dark hair spilled down her traditional white garb, striking a contrast against her flawless pale skin.

General Clerak was just behind her, cautiously surveying the space. Though no longer in service to the Kaian military, she still looked every bit the career soldier in a high-collared sweater and stiff jacket.

"Hello, my darling," Kavana said with a warm smile.

The magistrate pointed his stone towards them.

"Bailiffs! Arrest the intruders!"

"How'd you even get on the planet without me hearing about it?" Val asked.

Kavana raised her hands as the bailiffs surrounded her, their guns drawn.

"Don't worry, I've no intention of resisting. I simply came here to give something to my daughter."

"And be tried for sedition," said Val.

"I'm Palan, dear, not Kaian."

"You married the king of Kaia, you fall under our ruling."

"So you admit he was the rightful king?" Angela asked.

"No one said 'rightful,'" said Val. "But congratulations, you can have your mother keep you company from an adjoining cell."

"You'll never make any charges against me stick," Kavana said. "Not once my daughter's taken what's owed her. Here."

She drew a metal object from beneath her cloak and flung it towards the witness stand.

Val dove for it, but Angela's fingers found it first.

She quickly turned it in her grasp and pressed it to her forehead. Val had only moments to recognize the Crown of the

Five Point Star before Angela activated it, encasing her in the same armor her father had once worn into battle. The armor forming around her shattered her shackles, sending them to clattering to the floor.

Val stood before her, her jaw threatening to slacken. The bailiffs hurried Kavana and Clerak away.

"No..." Val breathed.

BOOK 5: DISCOVERY

CHAPTER 1

The broken shackles at her feet had barely stopped jangling.

Angela stood revealed to the courtroom, encased in the armor granted to her by the Crown of the Five Point Star. Ancient metal encircled her limbs, protected all joints and vital areas. The front of the helmet was forged from an expansion of the Crown itself.

The crowd in the courtroom collectively held its breath, unsure what to do. Many were too stunned to even move.

Val dropped her own Crown into place, activating her own armor, and leapt over the prosecutor's table, landing between Angela and the packed gallery.

"Stop," she demanded.

"No," said Angela.

"Stop, or you'll be stopped."

"Not until my mothers are released."

Val was undeterred.

"Take off the Crown and sit down. Final warning."

"You'll notice I've not made any move against you, or anyone," Angela said. "You're the aggressor here."

"You wearing that armor is an act of aggression."

"Release my mothers."

"They'll stand trial for their crimes, the same as you."

Angela took a step towards her.

"This trial is done."

She planted one foot on the railing of the witness box and launched herself into the air, over the defense's table where her would-be legal team still sat.

Val made a short hop into the air and gripped Angela's ankle, pulling her to the ground before she could make it into the spectators' box.

Chips of stone were sent skittering across the floor as Angela hit the ground, but the armor protected her completely. She scrambled gracelessly to her feet and squared up to Val.

The two exchanged a series of blows so quick that onlookers could barely keep up. The armor each wore granted them preternatural speed, though Angela's more powerful armor allowed her to strike harder.

Val called upon her years of training and made a quick shot for her opponent's kidneys. She was dismayed to find the punch deflected by a swift forearm set in her path. Seeing an opening on Angela's left side, Val swung again, but was once more denied proper contact.

As the two faced off, large swaths of the gallery members began shoving for the exit. Hundreds of bodies were still packed in and now sought escape. Others stayed behind, watching the spectacle as their peers pushed past on their way out.

Val took a jab straight at Angela. The younger woman's arms crossed up, catching Val's extended limb between them. Angela pushed back and steadied herself.

Past her adversary, she caught sight of Kavana and Clerak being hustled out of the room by the court bailiffs.

"No!"

She threw Val aside and took off after her mothers.

The queen had to take a moment to collect herself.

Making his way over from the bench seating, Bontu reached for her.

"Val..."

"I've got this."

"What do you need from me?"

"Get the kids out of here," Val instructed.

Jenneca started to object. "But…"

Val looked to her.

"And you get the grands out of here." She turned back to her guardian. "Then find Trainer. We need to get that Crown off of her and he knows how."

Bontu nodded, brought himself upright, and headed off. Val's children followed close behind.

CHAPTER 2

It was evening on whatever planet Donnie now called home. In the quaint little kitchen, he sat at the table with several of his security detail. They each held playing cards in their hand, with a few discarded onto the table itself.

Donnie tapped his cards against the tabletop.

Again.

He held the cards up and glanced them over.

He knocked them against the table yet again.

"You do know how to play this, don't you?" asked one of the guards.

"Of course I do." Donnie sneered. "If you're bored waiting, why don't you go get us some more snacks."

"No thanks, I'm not hungry."

Donnie lifted and shook his glass.

"How about something to drink, then?"

"You've got lemonade," another of the guards stated flatly.

"Something a little stronger?"

"You're underage."

"I think I deserve some consideration," Donnie said. "I'm a political prisoner, after all."

"Nope, just the regular kind. Now you gonna play?"

Donnie rapped his cards on the table once more.

He pushed the stack of chips in front of him towards the center.

"Yeah, I'm playing."

The guards all chuckled and 'ooh-ed.'

Donnie dropped his cards on the table, face up.

The second guard grabbed his slacking jaw. "Oh damn."

Donnie sat back with a satisfied grin.

Then the first guard dropped his cards.

"Oh damn, indeed," he said.

"Oh, shit," said another of them.

Donnie's face dropped.

The troopers all laughed as their commander scooped up the pile of chips.

"Okay," Donnie huffed, "one more."

"One more what?" the lead guard asked. "You're out, kid."

Donnie's fingers went to his wrist, fumbling a bit with the clasp on his thick gold bracelet before he was able to remove it and drop it in the center of the table.

"We'll play for this," he declared. "It belonged to my grandfather. It's worth a fortune."

"We're playing for chips here," the lead guard said. "Bragging rights. You've got no use for money, and I don't want to rob a kid."

"I dunno," one of his compatriots said, "the little shit kind of deserves to be cleaned out."

"That's not our call. Sorry kid. Better luck next time."

Dishes rattled as Donnie slammed his fists on the table, grabbed his bracelet, growled something indecipherable, and stormed off into the living space.

CHAPTER 3

V al burst into the castle hallway outside the courtroom.
There she found the bailiffs scattered on the floor,
unconscious or nursing wounds.

She took off running down the hall, following the trail of
disorder and the sounds of scuffling.

Former onlookers still crowded the corridor, a mass of
people that Val had to force her way through while trying not to
add to the damages of the day.

She came to a particularly dense throng crowding a corner
and began, as gently as she could, to move them out of her path.

"Move aside."

At the center of the grouping she found Kavana and Clerak
pressed against the stone wall, while Angela stood, her arms
spread, holding the rush of confused bodies in check.

"Back!" Angela shrieked. "Stay back!"

"Jeez." Val made it through to the small clearing.

"I said…" Angela gave Val a mighty shove, sending her
sprawling into the far wall. A number of onlookers were blasted
out of her path, skidding to the cold floor. Val's armored body
collided with the stone, sending a small smattering of dust and
freshly ground gravel into the air.

"Dammit." Val grunted.

"Stay back!" Angela's head snapped around as she
surveyed the chaotic passageway. "And that goes for all of you.
Not a finger on my mothers!"

Val brushed herself off as she rose to her feet.

"Back up. Everyone, give her space."

Angela's posture still didn't relax even as the crowd withdrew from her personal space. She stood coiled and ready to spring.

"Okay, what's your endgame here?" Val asked.

"What will happen..." said Kavana.

"No, not you. I'll get to you in a minute. Angela, what do you see happening here? Are you going to try to kill me now?"

"No," Angela said. "I... if I have to."

"I have no intention of forcing your hand here," Val said. "You seem upset."

"Of course she's..." Kavana began again.

"Can it. Angela, I get it. Mothers are a touchy subject around here. But until proven otherwise, you're still the accused in a trial, and there's been zero verdict giving you any kind of authority. So your mothers will have to be taken into custody."

"That won't happen," Angela said.

"I give you my word, no harm will come to them."

"The word of a murderer means very little to me," said Clerak.

"What about my word, Clerak?" Trainer could be seen over the top of the mass of people as he approached. Bontu was not far behind him. "I was your C.O. for how many years? Does my word still hold weight for you?"

"You're a fine officer, but known to be a lapdog of the royal family." Clerak glanced at Angela, who hadn't moved, hadn't flinched in some time. "Still, I don't wish any harm to come to my daughter." She approached Angela and placed a reassuring hand on her arm. "Angela, please relent."

Angela looked back over her shoulder before lifting the Crown on her face, retracting the armor. She did not fully remove the Crown, leaving it affixed to her forehead.

Members of the royal guard moved in and lead the three prisoners away. Angela was the last to follow along, staring Val down as they went.

CHAPTER 4

Donnie again sat at the white kitchen table, staring across at his primary guard. He only occasionally allowed his eyes to dart down to the cards in his hand.

He drew one of them and set it on the tabletop.

"One."

Another of the guards dealt him a single card from the top of the deck.

Donnie smiled.

"Bam."

He turned his hand around and swung his arms wide, back and forth, making sure that everyone present got a good look at the card faces.

"Okay." The lead guard dropped his cards, face up, on the table.

Donnie's face flushed instantly.

He slammed his cards down.

"Goddammit!"

The lead guard picked the bracelet from the center of the table and secured it around his wrist.

"We tried to warn you."

"Crap!"

"You're really not good at this game," said another of the guards. "Maybe that's why we weren't playing for money."

"Also because the kid doesn't have any money," said the dealer. "His mommy took it all away."

Donnie pushed away from the table and stomped off, brushing past the other guards as he went.

"Hey, watch it," one of them groused.

"No one likes a sore loser, Donnie." The lead guard smiled as he admired the piece of jewelry that newly adorned his arm.

CHAPTER 5

I t was not too long after Angela had been secured back in her cell that Val came looking for her.

She stopped and gazed at the bars that separated the two of them.

"The bailiffs all lived, if you care. A few broken bones, some blunt force trauma."

"Of course I care," Angela said plainly. "They're my subjects. I didn't want to have to hurt them."

"I'll bet. That leaves us at a bit of an impasse, doesn't it?"

"Beg pardon?"

"We have extra security stationed outside, but we both know that with that Crown you could get out of here anytime you wanted."

Angela didn't respond.

"So what's keeping you here? What's the plan now?" Val maneuvered to look her in the eye. "Do you even have one? Or did something put a hitch in it already?"

Angela sneered.

"That's it, isn't it? Your moms showed up, still not a hundred percent sure how you coordinated that, but they showed up at your trial. That was your moment of triumph, or it should have been. I can't believe they goofed something up, so it must have been you, wasn't it?" Val straightened herself back up. "What was it? Was it leaping into the gallery? Hurting those bailiffs? Look, I get it, I'm a mother myself."

"And some mother."

"You're worried... what? That you disappointed them?"

There wasn't much room in the cell for Angela to truly look away. In turning from her captor, she ended up facing straight at a stone wall.

"What does it hurt for you to talk to me?" Val asked.

"You're my enemy."

"I don't have to be." Val tried to force a smile. She backed away. "Okay. Well, if you decide you want to talk..."

"I want to see my mothers."

"I thought you might. And I'm willing to make that happen."

In spite of herself, Angela's eyes lit up.

"The only condition is, you have to surrender that crown."

The younger woman's heart sank.

"I didn't think so," Val said. "Worth a try, I guess. Let me know if you change your mind."

Bontu and Trainer waited some distance away, up another of the winding corridors of the wing of justice.

Val approached, in her usual poised way.

"How'd it go?" Bontu asked.

"About as well as you'd expect."

"I'd have expected the pair of you to bring the whole building down around our ears."

"Okay, so, maybe slightly better than that. We need to get that crown off of her. I am not comfortable with her keeping it."

Trainer shook his head.

"I suppose you're expecting me to do that."

"You're the expert."

"I was able to remove your Crown when you were unconscious, and even then it took time. And the bond with the Five Point crown is even stronger."

"Which brings up another very good point; how the hell

does she even have that thing?" Val asked.

"How else?" Bontu replied. "Magic."

"Very funny," said Val.

"I wasn't trying to be."

She sighed.

"How're the kids?"

"Strong, as ever," said Bontu.

"Good. That's good. I mean, really, they're probably all freaking the hell out, but…"

"I know. I'd worry about the effects this would be having on my little ones if I were in your place."

"Yeah, sorry, I'd ask how your kids are doing but we haven't got all day."

Bontu chuckled.

"So, what now?" he asked.

Val moved past the two men and headed up the hallway.

"Now we try to get some answers."

CHAPTER 6

In the late morning, Donnie made his way through the kitchen again. A small satchel was lashed across his back. He maneuvered deftly through the space, around the furniture and fixtures, making not a sound as he went. Years of Trainer's tutelage were paying off.

He slowly, carefully gripped the knob on the back door and swung it open without so much as a hint of a creek.

On his way out of the house, he was sure not to let the door slam behind him. Not even a 'click' from the latch bolt snapping back into place.

He did, however, hear the distinctive sound of a gun sliding from its holster as soon as he was out.

"Where do you think you're going?" the guard asked.

Donnie turned to face him, not raising his hands or showing any outward sign of distress.

"Just wanted to stretch my legs," he said.

"You seem a little unclear as to the meaning of 'house arrest.' Back in the house."

"Come on. Who'm I going to hurt?"

"It's not my place to worry about that. I just do what I'm ordered. And that means keeping you inside the house at all times."

"At least tell me what planet we're on," Donnie said. "Is there a town nearby or something that you don't want me getting to? A port? I need out of this place for a little bit."

"You are here for the rest of your life. Don't go getting stir crazy already. You won't have anything to look forward to."

The guard followed as Donnie sullenly slunk back towards the door.

"Come on, man."

"Also, that tracker is tamperproof," the guard said. "You're not as smart as you think you are."

CHAPTER 7

Kavana shifted in her seat.

It was hard, unyielding. Not at all what she'd grown up accustomed to. Not even as fine as what suspects brought into the palace typically received.

Her wrists being chained to the table in front of her didn't help in finding a comfortable position.

The room around her was small and bleak. In the years she'd spent on the run, she'd seen her share of bleak, but it was rarely so dull and featureless.

Val entered, removed her cloak, and carefully hung it on a hook near the door.

She sat down across the table from her prisoner.

"Hello, Kavana."

"Valentina."

The years had been kind to Kavana. Or perhaps it was some of that magic for which she was so famous. If Val hadn't known better, she could have passed for Angela's sister, rather than her mother.

"I'm sure you know that I've been trying to arrange this very chat for quite some time."

Kavana may have been a practiced manipulator, but Val could see through the false smile on her face.

"I know. You'd think someone with your resources would have an easier time programming her social calendar."

"So, that's how you want to play this?"

"I'd like to, bu-ut..." She sighed. "Clerak won't give you anything. She doesn't know the specifics of much of it anyway. And Angela..."

"Angela is currently on trial for, if you can believe it, theft of my Crown." Val tapped the metal band wrapped around her forehead. "But I guess she wouldn't even need it, would she?"

"Of course this was never about your knockoff headgear."

"How'd you manage that little trick, anyway?"

"You mean with the Five Point crown?" Val nodded to her. "The physical Crown itself was lost when you shot Angelo into that star. But the energy, that could be reclaimed, imbued into a newly forged home."

"How? No mage on Kaia knows the secrets of the old Order."

"I guess I've just got a knack for recruiting the right talent."

"Like when you recruited Angelo?"

"I didn't recruit Angelo."

"Sure. He wouldn't have known it, but I've read the records of what went on around here while I was searching for the other Crowns. You played him and you got everything you wanted."

"I loved Angelo," Kavana said. "I don't suppose you'd know what that's like."

"Oh, you got me. I'm aromantic. Way to go for, you know, going after something everyone in the kingdom has known for seventeen years."

"Not quite that long, I don't think."

"My love life, or lack thereof, is not on the table today."

"Very well," Kavana said. "I'd like to see my daughter."

"I bet you would." Val smiled at her.

"What about my wife?"

"You're a prisoner of the royal guard. You don't get visitation rights. Unless you're seeking legal counsel."

"We both know I'm not doing that. No rush there, anyway. You won't put me on trial until you've finished with Angela, and by then I'll be looking at a full pardon. Or, maybe not a pardon, since it will be recognized that I've committed no crimes."

"What about murdering the former vizier?" Val asked.

"Are you still worrying about that?"

"There's no statute of limitations on murder."

"Yes, well, I trust my daughter to look after me. Can you say the same about each of your children?"

"It would help your daughter if you'd cooperate," Val stated.

"I'm sorry, has this conversation not been illuminating for you?"

Val rose up from the table and swung her cloak back onto her shoulders.

"Keep playing, Kavana. Make me regret letting you go all those years ago."

"I believe I've already succeeded in that." As best she could with her fettered wrists, she waved as Val left the room.

CHAPTER 8

Evening fell on the small house on the unknown planet.

The lead guard and one of his subordinates sat at the kitchen table again, a spread of bread, meats, and cheeses before them. Each man had a bowl of steaming creamy substance as well.

Their third compatriot entered, carrying a tray upon which sat a bowl and plate, each containing the appropriate food stuffs for the vessel.

"Still nothing?" the seated guard asked.

"Nope. That's day two of his hunger strike now."

"So what do we do? Message the queen and tell her her kid isn't eating?"

"He'll eat when he's hungry enough," the lead guard said.

CHAPTER 9

Upon entering her sitting room, Val found Bontu, Trainer, and her children waiting. Along with them was John, nuzzled up on the sofa next to Bontu.

"How'd it go?" Bontu asked.

"How do you think?"

"That bad, huh?"

"And how is Aunt Kavana?" Jenneca asked.

"Please don't call her that," Val said. "She's not your aunt, anyway, she's... oh, God, she's mine."

"So she'd be my great aunt."

"Our family tree is disgusting," Val said.

"What about Clerak?" Trainer asked.

"What about her?" Val asked.

"Did she have anything to say?"

"I haven't spoken with her. I'm not sure I'll even bother."

"I could speak with her," Trainer offered.

"If you want to, I won't stop you. But we're dealing with the supernatural elements of what's been happening for the last seventeen years. That's not really her area of expertise."

"She's been married to someone adept in manipulating those with supernatural talents for the better part of two decades. It might be worth seeing what she knows."

"Fine. Like I said, I won't stop you."

"What about Naoke?" Jenneca asked. "Er, Angela?"

"What about her?" her mother replied.

"What sort of, you know, vibe did you get from her?"

"Vibe? Where did you pick up language like that?"

"From the grands."

"Of course," said Val. "Angela is... she's not your concern, honey."

"I just... I always got along with her well."

"Until she accused you of abusing her in open court," Val reminded her.

"I told you, she was lying about that."

"Even so, she's clearly not who you thought she was."

"Should we, I don't know, should we try talking to her?" Neva asked.

"I've already tried," said Val.

"I meant us. We're closer to her age."

"And you've had interrogation training?"

"I didn't mean to interrogate her. I just meant... never mind."

"No, I'm sorry. I haven't been trying to interrogate her, either. But we need information. Or, I do. You kids honestly don't need to be here. Neva, if you'd rather be with your parents right now, you can go. Should, even."

"No, I... it's more proper that I'm here, isn't it?"

"Probably, yeah. I've never been big on doing what's proper myself."

"And now you're on the cusp of losing your empire to a spoiled child and a pair of traitors," Bontu noted. Val glared at him. "What. I'm tactless. I didn't grow up around people."

"You know it's long past time you stopped using that as an excuse."

Bontu shrugged.

"So, what about Neva's idea?" Jenneca asked.

"What about it?" asked Val.

"Should one of us try talking to her? Or, more than one of us? For safety."

"No," Val said. "Look, Angela is unstable. I can't tell you how many different moods I've seen from her the handful of times I've tried talking with her. Plus she has the Crown now. That makes her dangerous."

"Neva could take the Crown. The Ten Point one, when she goes to talk to her, I mean. Neva could take it with her."

"Or me," Sanke piped up.

"Or me," said Joseph.

"Well, sure," said Jenneca.

"No one is taking the Crown until I'm dead," said Val. "When that happens, you all can do whatever you want with Angela. Sound good?" The kids grumbled at her. "Glad we had this talk."

In another interrogation room in the justice wing, it was Clerak who sat shackled to a table.

The door opened and Trainer forced his way through the frame.

"Oh, it's you," Clerak remarked. "Your queen not up to doing her own dirty work?"

"Not interested." He took the seat across from her. "She already spoke to your wife and daughter. It seems she doesn't figure you have anything of worth to add."

"Am I supposed to feel insulted by that?" she asked. "Goaded into a reaction?"

"I won't tell you what to feel. But I think we both know you're adept enough to know more than they let on."

"You've no idea."

"I think I do. I'm not here to insult you or to underestimate you." His voice rumbled like a drum.

"I mean, you've no idea about any of this," she said. "None of you do."

"Then maybe you'd care to enlighten me. For old times' sake?"

"We were teacher and student, not lovers. Speaking of old times, how old are you now, anyway?"

"That's not..."

"You expect me to answer your questions, you could answer a simple one of mine."

"I'm not here to play games with you," he stated.

"Nor I with you. But I've spent the last seventeen years married to a woman who near-constantly plays games. I've grown used to it."

"Perhaps you'd like to tell me about that."

"About my wife? We're not friends, you and I."

"You respected me enough to trust that I'll keep my word that no harm would come to you or your family. You can respect me enough to speak plainly with me."

"That wasn't my idea," Clerak said.

"What wasn't?"

"Angela surrendering herself, letting us all be taken prisoner."

"You're the one who instructed your daughter to relent."

"Only to avoid turmoil on the road that Kavana had set us upon. Or... oop, no, that would be telling."

"What would?"

Clerak gave a hearty laugh.

"Oh, this is fun. I'm too often on the receiving end of these sorts of things. It's a refreshing change of pace to be able to string someone else along."

"I'm asking you to help your family here," Trainer said. "I'd think you'd want to be more cooperative."

"You should be more concerned with your own family."

"You know full well I never had a family."

"Are you sure about that? I know what sort of activities go on behind the scenes in the castle. At any rate, I was speaking of the queen and her ilk. You have a father's affection for them."

"Hardly."

"If you didn't, you wouldn't have sided against my husband all those years ago."

"I sided with Valentina because she was in the right," Trainer said. "Don't forget I trained Angelo as well. He was a sick man."

"Besmirch my husband's name all you wish, you still won't get a rise out of me. I wonder if, after all these years, the hurt hasn't dulled a bit. I still carry it with me, and I won't forget your role in things, but it doesn't ache the same as it used to. Having others to live for helped, I suppose."

"And now you and all those others are in jail. That must hurt in its own way."

"You've no idea who or what I've been living for," she said. "My wife and daughter, certainly. But oh, it's been a long time. To watch my looks fade away. That's not easy in itself, being married to such a fine young woman. Kavana could still have nearly any man or woman she wanted, while me... being a mother fills me with a pride I cannot describe, but I'm not unaware that I'm old enough to be my daughter's grandmother. And all those years, Kavana insisting on playing the 'long game.' It amused me at first, that such a naïve young wisp of a thing thought she knew anything of strategy. But I'll admit, she was sharper than I gave her credit for."

"How so?"

"Ah. That would be telling. I'll keep my love's secrets, thank you."

"I can help you, Clerak," he said, "if you'll cooperate. You were a general before all this. You could have a military tribunal, rather than a civilian trial. The sentence is sure to be much lighter."

"I've just wailed on about my advancing years and you think I care a wit for the harshness of my sentence?" she asked. "Tribunal or trial, I'll not live long enough to see the end of my prison stay."

"It's not lost on me that you've also mentioned how young your wife is. Not to mention your daughter, not yet out of her teenage years. How will they fair in court, I wonder?"

"Once again, you were a fine instructor but you make a poor student. I'm not going to see the inside of a prison cell, nor will Kavana or Angela. I will live to see my daughter on the throne, though. That will be a satisfying day."

"No, you won't," Trainer said. "The law is clear."

"Is it?"

Trainer nodded. "This sham of a trial will end with Val's right to rule affirmed."

"Will it indeed? I'm not sure I'd be so confident, were I in your place."

"But you're not," he said. "You were never going to be, on any meaning."

"Oh, you don't have any idea how wrong you are, do you?"

"I'm not wrong," he said.

"Wait and see. See what becomes of you, what becomes of your family, what's become of your allies."

"Alright, I think we're done here."

"One of us is."

She didn't budge as he stood and left her alone in the room.

CHAPTER 10

The three guards lay on the table, doubled over. None moved a muscle, not even a rising of the chest to draw breath.

Donnie smirked down at them as he moved casually through the kitchen.

"Who's clever now?"

He opened the back door and made for the guards' ship, sitting across the field from the house.

A single shot rang out from the surrounding trees.

Donnie dropped to the ground.

CHAPTER 11

Trainer rejoined Val and Bontu, who were the only ones remaining in the sitting room by the time she returned.

"So, was your interrogation as productive as you'd hoped?" Val asked.

"As I'd hoped? No. As I'd expected, well..."

Bontu looked at his comm device.

"Val, you're being summoned," he said.

"Oh?" She moved to the comm unit hidden within the bureau against the wall. The glow from the screen illuminated her face, though the open doors of the cabinet hid the contents of the screen from the others. "Hey."

"I didn't expect to hear from you," she said, followed by, "You are?" and then, "Oh. I... thank you for telling me."

"What is it?" Bontu asked as the cast light faded.

"My son is dead."

Bontu rose from his seat and moved towards her.

"Val..."

Any moment between the pair was interrupted as barrister Ulcen Dorrster entered.

"My queen, er, we've news."

"Is it... can it wait? I'm sorry, I..."

"I'm afraid not. The magistrate has yet to rule, but I've been consulting with the Order of Meridian and the royal record keepers. We've regrettably come to the unfortunate conclusion that Angela's claim may in fact be legitimate."

"You can't be serious," said Val.

"She possesses the Crown of the Five Point Star, handed down to her by her father."

"That's not..." Desperation crept into her voice.

"Technicalities. I'm sorry, but a victory in court is no longer a certainty. The law states that rule of the empire belongs to whomever possesses the Crown. The Ten Point Crown was never legitimized into law."

"We never... the Five Point crown was destroyed," Val said.

"It appears that has been undone," said Ulcen.

Bontu checked his comm device again.

"Val."

"What, Bontu?"

He met her eyes, a look somewhere between confusion and worry on what could be seen of his face behind his overgrown beard.

"There's a Palan fleet approaching Kaia."

"A what?"

"It dropped out of fold-space outside the system and is approaching at sublight speed," Bontu said.

"Why in the hell... okay, get me King Stelleco on comms. I don't care what time it is on Palan. This is batshit insane."

Bontu nodded and went to work on his comm device.

"Queen Valentina," said Ulcen.

"What?" Val snapped.

"You know I am loyal to the crown, but I'm not sure how to proceed here. I cannot say with certainty that you're the queen..."

"I'm on the throne now. Angela's in a cell, and she's going to stay there until... dammit, I should get down there."

"Val?" Trainer asked.

"If she decides to make a move now, no one else will be able to stop her." Val rushed from the room, her cloak billowing behind her.

CHAPTER 12

Val found Angela still sat behind bars within the justice wing's holding facility.

"You're still here," Val said.

"Where else would I be?"

"You never know with your family."

"Here's the thing; I already know how this is going to go," Angela said.

"You see the future now?"

"Not me. But someone wiser and more powerful. My mothers never let me practice the mystic arts."

"Since almost everyone they know who tried is long dead, that's probably a good idea."

"And one of them knew things. Without him I might not even be here."

"What sort of things did this person allegedly know?"

"That without me, Kaia would fall. It still might. Andor's bloodline isn't strong enough to save it. But Angelo's is. My father's is. And I'm all that's left. Me and my Crown."

Bontu hurried into the room behind them.

"Val."

"Do you have Stelleco on comms?"

"You'd need something more powerful than one of our arrays for that," Bontu said. "Stelleco is dead."

"Beg pardon?" Val asked.

"He's…"

"I heard you, I just... how did he die? Was it... Kavana?"

"They're saying it was just age," Bontu said. "But, his eldest son has taken the throne."

"That's, ah, Domnock. Can you raise him?"

"I've got their communications minister standing by but..."

"But they've got a fleet in our space," Val said.

"That as well, yes, but that's not all. The fleet says it's here to acknowledge the ascension of Kaia's new queen."

Red flashed across Val's face. Her eyes narrowed and her delicate brow furrowed.

"We don't have a new queen."

"Your closest ally seems to be under the impression that you do," said Angela.

"She's right," Bontu said. "And if the intergalactic community recognizes Angela as the new queen..."

"They're setting us up for another civil war," Val reasoned.

"Maybe not just civil," said Bontu. "The last time Kaia waged war against itself, it left us open to attack from the Artondy. If we repeat those same mistakes..."

"We open ourselves up to challenges from any and every star empire out there," Val said. She turned to Angela. "Is this what you call saving Kaia?"

"I didn't write the prophecy, and I don't claim to fully understand it. I'm just trying to play my part. It seems to me that the choice is yours. Abdicate, or leave Kaia to whatever fate awaits it. Is that a chance you want to leave our empire to?"

BOOK 6: DISMISSED
PART 1

CHAPTER 1

Val strode resolutely through the halls of the palace. Bontu and Trainer kept apace, with a contingent of attendants struggling behind.

"Get me Domnock on comms, now," Val said.

"I've already got Barnord working on it," Bontu replied.

"Good. We need to head this off."

"I'm aware of that."

General Bly rushed towards them from the oncoming direction.

"M'lady."

"What is it? We're all kind of busy here at the moment."

The general turned to keep stride with the queen and her retinue.

"Understood. We're receiving word from our outpost at the Ao Sea."

"Our... why?" Val asked.

"That's why I came right to find you," said Bly. "They're reporting Palan ships touching down."

"By whose authority?" Val asked.

"They're saying by the queen's."

Val's eyes drifted closed for a moment. Then she let out a growl.

She turned to Bontu.

"Domnock. Now."

He nodded and headed away.

"What shall we do, my queen?" Bly asked. "About the Palans?"

"For now, establish a perimeter and keep them contained. I don't want to engage in a galactic war if I don't have to. But if I have to, I will fight them, and I will win."

Val's cloak flowed behind her as she continued up the corridor.

Along the coast of the Ao Sea, Kaian citizens could only watch as Palan warships descended from above and made their landing in the lake itself. Mammoth craft, dark, imposing, and angular, came down, cracking the water's surface, sending spray high into the air. Waves were sent roiling towards the sandy coastline as one behemoth after another nestled its way into the Kaian waters.

The royal communications room was sheltered high in the castle. It was the same stone as the rest of the place, yet without any of the warmth that defined the residence. Cold in both color and climate. Sterile.

Bontu leaned over Barnord, a much smaller man who worked the glowing controls, as Val entered.

"Do you have him?"

Barnord looked at his queen, sheepish. He had been with the royal family for years and was still intimidated by her presence.

Bontu stood tall.

"You're not going to like the answer."

"I never like to be told what I'll like or not," she said.

Bontu shrugged.

"He's refusing to speak with you."

Val's face flashed red.

"What?"

"I told you you wouldn't like it. He says he'll only speak with the recognized scion of the Kaian Empire. One guess as to who he's referring to."

"Who he's referring to is currently in one of our holding cells," Val said, "and she is not the recognized ruler of the empire."

"All this has been explained to the Palan comms station," said Bontu, "but they're not putting us through to the palace."

Val sighed as she pushed her hair back.

"Move."

Barnord looked up at her.

"M'lady?"

Val made a brushing gesture through the air with her waving hands.

Barnord slid away from his station, making space for Val to hunch over it.

The Palan throne room was not as large or extravagant as its Kaian counterpart. It still featured the main seat, pushed off to one side of the room, raised on a pedestal. That pedestal didn't rise as high as the Kaian throne, and shared the dais with a less opulent seat for the monarch's partner.

The chamber itself held a different shape. Where everything in the Kaian palace was built around circular design, the Palan throne room was harshly squared off, wider than it was long.

Along one wall was set a lengthy table, and upon that table was set a small feast for the monarchy and their attendants throughout the day.

Domnock sat upon the throne. He was tall, athletic, with a militaristic style of dress, blue and gold. His wife, a woman every bit the social butterfly as her husband, sat by his side.

Attendants went about their business in the space, making sure everyone's plates and cups were full to their liking.

A general stood beside the king, leaning over to converse with his lordship.

A flash of light abruptly permeated the room as Val's holographic visage formed before the throne.

The king, queen, generals, advisors, all were thrown back, nearly dropping their various platters and chalices. One attendant nearly spun to the ground, having been walking through the spot where the projection had blinked to life.

"There you are," There was a slight tinny rasp to the sound the projection made.

"What... how dare you?" Domnock demanded. He made no effort to rise from his throne.

Val's arms folded.

"I've currently got dozens of unauthorized Palan ships on and around my throne world. Let's not start talking about who is daring what here."

Domnock's eyes narrowed at the sight.

"How did you even..."

"I was a special operative long before I was a queen. Now tell your people to pull back, immediately."

Domnock finally stood to face Val's ghostly form.

"I will do no such thing. The Palan fleet is there at the behest of the true queen of Kaia."

"Look, Domnock, your father and I always enjoyed a civil relationship."

The king paced around the intrusive image in his presence.

"You openly mocked him at every available opportunity."

"Okay, but to be fair, I do that with everyone I don't think is smart enough to catch on."

"And don't speak of my father at all."

"Do you also recall that he took every available opportunity to proposition me? He enjoyed our little tit-for-tats a bit too much, I think."

"The warmth has barely left his corpse before you seek to besmirch his name?"

"And you seek to undo his strongest alliance," Val said.

"You know I've never liked you," Domnock said coldly. "My father may have played off the harshness of your attitude, but I never have. Nor have I forgotten the friendly family visits from Prince Angelo."

"Angelo didn't hesitate to wage war against Palan as soon as his bride, your baby sister I'd remind you, fluttered her eyelashes at him," Val said.

"And it is for my dear sister's sake that I send aid to Kaia now, her and my niece's."

"You haven't seen Kavana in almost two decades, and I doubt you've ever even met Angela."

"Do you not think that wounds me?" Domnock's hand went to his breast. "Family is everything to me. I must try to mend my relationship with my sister, and forge one with her child, if even the slightest opportunity presents itself."

"Uh-huh. And in what universe is invading a sovereign planet considered 'aid?'" Val asked.

"I was requested by the rightful queen to help her preserve the peace during a difficult transfer of power."

"There's no transfer of power going on," Val said.

"There's more of that arrogance I've always hated."

"Alright. I don't know what the outcome of all this will be. But I do know it's not going to be one that you like. I can promise you that."

Domnock leaned in towards her.

"Get out of my throne room, princess."

Val's nostrils flared as her image faded.

The king looked around. Everywhere, attendants and advisors stood rigidly in place.

"And someone figure out how she got in here in the first place. I want our security patched immediately."

CHAPTER 2

"**S**o, did that go as well as you'd hoped?" Bontu asked as the transmission cut off.

"I didn't have much hope," Val said. She stepped back from the holo-transcriber. "I was more trying to get Domnock's measure."

"And?"

"And he's going to be trouble. How are things going in Ao?"

"The perimeter you've requested has been established," Bontu informed her.

"I'm sensing a 'but' coming."

"Hehe. You said 'butt.'"

"Bontu..."

"Sorry, you know I can't help myself. The 'but,' and I won't tell you if you'll like this or not, but the 'but' is that there are rumblings amongst the ranks of Angelo loyalists rearing their ugly heads."

Val leaned herself against the comm panel.

"Dammit."

"I don't understand how," Bontu said. "You did a pretty thorough job purging any Angelo loyalists back in the day."

"From the leadership, yeah. But I was nice enough to offer amnesty to lower-ranked soldiers who were just following orders. I guess that's come back to bite me in the ass. Some of them have probably worked their way up to leadership positions by now."

"It's about the only way the Palans could have gotten to Kaia without our planetary defenses blowing them all to hell."

"There is that, yeah."

"What do you want to do about it?" Bontu asked.

"This is getting too dangerous," said Val. "I want to enact Plan B."

"I thought you might. Preparations have been made." He held up a data pad for her. "We just need you to select a destination spot from the list..."

Val reached out and tapped the screen.

Bontu turned it back towards himself and looked it over.

His face scrunched up.

"Um, that's..."

"I'm aware of where it is."

"...not on the list."

"That's kind of the point."

Bontu sighed. "It's going to be harder to secure."

"Yeah, but fewer people would ever even think to look there."

Bontu's eyebrows arched.

"If you think that's wisest."

"I do. And I'm the queen."

Angela sat on the bench in her holding cell, folded in on herself.

Her stomach let out an unholy racket.

"I dare say they've forgotten to feed me."

She stood and looked around as far as she could see through the bars around her.

"Now what could be distracting them, I wonder."

Val looked down from the window in her sitting room.

"Oh. Hey. This is familiar."

Behind her, Bontu made his way into the room.

"So you've seen the protestors."

"Yeah. They don't seem to be in total agreement just yet. Some are demanding my abdication, others just want me to 'Free Angela.'"

"This is what you get for being gentle with them all those years ago."

She turned away from the window, from the sight of the crowd gathered below at the castle gates.

"I was gentle, but I never gave in to their demands," she said. "And it's not like I'm going to now, either."

"Hrm. I was kind of hoping you'd let me go disperse the crowd."

"No, Bontu."

"You never let me have any fun."

Val sighed.

"Assaulting our citizens isn't 'fun.' Or it shouldn't be your idea of it, anyway."

"Just a bit wouldn't hurt," he said.

"It literally would."

"Well."

"We need to keep our focus where it belongs," she said.

"That being?"

"Domnock and the Palans. And Angela. And Kavana and Clerak."

"That doesn't sound like focus," he said.

"I know. We've got too many plates spinning."

"Yes we do."

"Not literally."

He patted his belly. "I thought we were discussing dinner."

"You can go eat if you want," she said. "I've got stuff to do."

His arms dropped to his sides.

"If you've got stuff to do, then we've got stuff to do."

The Palan throne room had become a flurry of activity. The attendants who'd previously muddled through their days now rushed about, along with new contingents of military personnel.

Domnock, though, sat upon the throne, servants bringing him platters of food and keeping his drink full.

"Has there been any word from my sister?" he asked.

"No, sire," said a general. "Though your sister has hardly proven herself to be, ah, reliable."

"I disagree," Domnock said. "She is self-serving, arrogant, conniving, but she's proven to be nothing but reliable in these things."

"I don't want to question the wisdom of your grace, but, ah..."

"Why am I trusting Kavana if she is indeed all those things?"

"That does seem to be the question on everyone's mind," said the general.

"Whose mind?"

The general tensed up, his face going pallid.

"No matter," Domnock said. "Yes, she is all those things, but she is my sister, and I fully meant what I told Valentina. And I have missed her. If there's any hope of reconciliation after all this time, I owe it to myself to grasp it. Tightly, and not let go unless I am forced to."

"I pray, my liege, that you not find yourself forced to do anything you don't wish to."

"Your concern is noted," Domnock said. "Now, where are we on Kaia?"

"We are, that is, if you are asking literally, our positioning hasn't changed. Our ships' landings have been confined to the Ao Sea on the planet's far side."

"That's fine."

"Anchoring continues abreast. We can deploy our smaller ships at any time."

"Good. Now if only Kavana would be in contact we would

know when and where to deploy them."

"If I may, sire, we can safely assume that a show of force on the capitol will be at some point necessary. Unless we're expecting Queen Valentina to surrender."

"We're not expecting that, and don't give her any royal title," said Domnock. "All communication of any kind is to proceed with the expectation that Angela is the rightful queen."

"Of course, sir. Forgive my slip of the tongue."

"That's alright."

"But as I was saying, we can safely assume that any action we take would be against the capitol city of Olivert. It may be prudent to ready our forces to move in that direction."

"That's part of the beauty of this small bit of planning we've done," said Domnock.

"Sire?"

"Do you know why the Ao Sea was chosen as a landing zone for our forces?" the king asked.

"I was not privy those discussions," the general said. "I assumed it had some level of strategic value."

"The Ao Sea is on the exact opposite side of the planet from Olivert. Precisely, to the very spot our ships touched down. It would take Valentina the longest amount of time possible to deploy forces from the capitol."

"Yes, sire, but wouldn't that also then make it the longest possible journey from landing to Olivert?"

"In every direction, yes. There's no singular route for the false queen to fortify against us."

"And we're certain their forces will be coming from Olivert?"

"Everything I know of Valentina tells me that she'll insist on leading any campaign herself. That makes Olivert the biggest target and the biggest threat."

"I'm not sure…"

Domnock glared at him.

"Never mind," the general said. "Nothing important."

"Good."

The king plucked some fruit from a nearby tray and popped it into his mouth.

CHAPTER 3

The hangar beneath the castle grounds was the birthplace of many adventures in Val's life. It was there that she and her allies set off on any number of quests, from dethroning her uncle to hunting mystic relics.

Now it was her family's turn. They gathered in the gleaming metal field, loading up one of the long royal cruisers.

Sanke was the last to arrive, hurrying in with a suitcase in hand.

"All packed?" Val asked.

An attendant took the case from the princess and added it to the skiff of luggage being loaded.

"Thank you," she said before turning to her mother. "Um, yeah. What's going on?"

"You all are going on a little trip." The warmth of excitement overtook Val's tone.

"Yeah, but where?" asked Joseph.

"You'll like it there," Val insisted. "There's a baby dragon for you to play with."

Sanke grew pale.

"You're sending us to a nature preserve?"

"Don't worry," her mother said, "you'll have plenty of security with you."

"That... might not sound as comforting as you think it does," said Catherine.

"I'm aware of how it sounds," said Val. "They're big kids,

they know what the universe is like. Now, watch out for John when you get there. You know how fearless he is, but there are all sorts of things on that planet that could eat him and then any of you."

"Couldn't you at least try to be a little comforting?" Catherine asked.

"Why are we all going?" asked Jason.

"Remember when you first came to Kaia, and I had you stay with Bontu?" Val asked. Jason shuddered. Bontu cracked a jagged smile. "This is much worse. I need you all safe so I can focus on fixing this."

"What if you can't?" Joseph asked.

"Joseph." Catherine chided him.

"No, it's alright," Val said. "Like I said, they're big kids, and hopefully I've done a decent enough job raising them. If I can't fix this, which I'm pretty sure I can, but if I can't, then you'll all be targets. Listen to Trainer, and he'll do his best to keep you alive."

"Aw, man, Trainer's coming?" asked Joseph.

"It was either him or Bontu..." said Val.

"Bontu," her children replied in unison.

"...and Bontu's place, as guardian, is at my right hand."

"Aww." The children groaned as one.

"I know." Val took Joseph by the shoulders, looked him in the eye, and kissed his forehead. "Be good, stay safe."

She kissed Sanke, then Jenneca. Jenneca especially was tightlipped and scowly.

Then Val came to Neva and her parents. She gripped the girl by the arms and looked into her eyes, holding for a moment before pulling her in and wrapping her up firmly.

No more words passed as Val placed a hand on each of the elder Nuw's shoulders and forced a reassuring smile to her face. More than half a life practicing deception had made such a gesture almost effortless, regardless of what was happening in her mind.

The group boarded the ship. Val and Bontu stood and watched it move out towards daylight, holding resolutely in place as the force from the engines slapped at them. Once the jet wash subsided, the pair headed back into the castle.

Palan ships continued their descent into the Ao Sea. They'd begun grouping together in a tight formation, locking their hulls and connecting via their airlocks.

Val had sent Bontu off to work on some preparations. She hadn't mentioned where she'd be, but he knew to find her in the sitting room.

"Val?" he asked upon entering. "Are you alright?"

She raised her head. Tears streamed from her eyes; a different, fouler sort of fluid ran from her nose.

"No. No, I'm very much not. My oldest son is dead, my planet's being invaded. I'm so not alright that I had to send my entire family off-world, knowing that if things go south, which they could for a million different reasons, I may never see them again."

Her cousin rubbed the back of his head and stepped towards her.

"But things could also go... uh, north?"

"That's not a saying."

"How does anyone keep track of these things?"

Val shrugged and gave an ugly sniffle.

"As for Donnie... well, all I can say is that you still have three children left," Bontu said. "Or four? Plus the others in hiding, but, um, we have to stay strong for them. And for the kingdom."

"I know," Val said. "I was just giving myself one moment where I didn't have to be so strong. It can be hard being strong all the time."

"I have not found that to be the case."

CHAPTER 4

Angela reclined on the prison bench, one foot up, one dangling in the wind. She stared at the wall, at nothing in particular.

She sat upright a moment before Kavana appeared in the doorway. She barely darkened it as she rushed into room.

"Angela."

"Mother."

Angela was already up, hurrying to the bars.

"You heard me coming?" Kavana asked.

"Of course."

"'Of course.' You say that as though anyone would have done so."

"Anyone who mum trained." She reached through the bars and hugged her mother.

"And I'm sure that Crown that gives you superhuman senses didn't help at all?"

"Well..."

"Oh, I have missed you."

"I've missed you too, mother."

"Now, come along, dear."

Her daughter withdrew from the embrace and pulled back into the shadowy enclosure.

"No."

"Beg pardon, young lady?"

"I'm not leaving. Why would I?"

"Because you are the queen of Kaia. You do not belong in a cage."

"No, I belong on the throne. I'm going nowhere until my title is acknowledged. Legally."

"Sweetie," Kavana's voice had a touch of exasperation to it, "the castle mightn't be safe for much longer."

"What do you mean?"

"You'll find my brother is quite mad. He's been aching for the chance to prove himself against your predecessor for some time. Until she abdicates, is driven off, or is in the ground, no place she inhabits will be safe from Domnock. Well, that might not be entirely true. He's batty enough he might have her taxidermied and mounted in the trophy room."

Angela balked. "Call him off, then! You're the one who got him to come here."

"Oh, he's not here. He'd never risk himself."

"His forces then, I mean."

"I doubt that's possible. As I said, he's quite mad. Mad both as in mentally unwell and angry. I'd nearly forgotten how obsessive he can be when he doesn't get his way."

She let out a breathy chuckle.

Clerak appeared in the entryway.

"What are you two playing at in here?" she asked. "We need to get moving."

"Oh, Angela says she's not coming," said Kavana.

"Then the two of us have to get on," said Clerak.

"Is that all you have to say?" Kavana gestured to Angela. "Your daughter is locked in a cell with the means to escape and she says she's going to remain there."

"She's not a child anymore. She's capable of making her own decisions." Clerak took Kavana's pouting face in her hands. "We raised her well. Trust in that. But the two of us are already fugitives. We need to be going."

"Yes," Angela said eagerly. "Go, mother. Please. Your plan requires your freedom. Mine requires my captivity."

Kavana sighed.

"Very well then."

She took Clerak's hand. They headed for the door.

Briefly, she allowed herself to turn back.

"I surely hope you know what you're doing."

"Of course she does." Clerak stopped and smiled. "She's her mother's keen mind."

That caused Kavana to grin as the pair of them disappeared into the shadows of the looming outer corridor.

CHAPTER 5

T he royal cruiser flew along, surrounded by escort ships. Though the nature of their mission was secret, the cruiser still bore the royal colors upon its hull.

Most of the royal family gathered in a plush living room aboard the ship.

Cruisers like this were not like the castle back home. While that structure was ancient and traditional in its appearance, ships in the family's service were regularly refreshed and replaced. The quarters and common areas were quite luxurious; they were also very modern in décor. The carpeting that adorned the floors would have seemed distinctly out of place in the old world aesthetic of the castle. The furniture, though very comfortable, lacked the antique charm of home.

Sanke nibbled on a snack. Trainer sat reclined off to one side, reading from a data pad.

Catherine stood by a side port, waving enthusiastically outward.

"Why do you do that?" her husband asked.

"Do what?" asked Catherine.

"Wave to the escort ships."

"It only seems polite to acknowledge them."

"Did they wave back?"

"I don't know, I can't really see from here."

She moved to a nearby console, humming to herself as she

worked the controls.

Music started playing, something from her old life on Earth. Her son had loved musicals, and she'd enjoyed sharing them with Val when they'd met. It was something Val was happy to pass down to her own children.

Catherine sang along. Sanke and Joseph joined in.

"Ooh, everybody sing." She looked to Trainer. "You too, Mr. Trainer."

"I, ah, don't know the words," he said.

Catherine held out a data pad containing a song book to him.

"Here you go."

He looked down at it.

"Alright, then I just don't want to."

"Oh." Catherine drew the book back. She looked around the room, at the pair of teenagers lounging on the couches. "Where's Jenneca? This song is her favorite."

"No," said Sanke, "it was mom's favorite."

"And Jenneca always took after mom," said Joseph.

"I don't think it's her favorite anymore," Sanke said.

"Don't tell me she outgrew show tunes?" Catherine tsked.

"No," Sanke replied, "I think she's just into stuff that's more modern. And Kaian."

"Oh. No, that's good. It helps her build her own identity," Catherine said.

"Yeah."

"Is she doing okay?" Catherine asked. "All around, I mean. The last few weeks have been hard on her."

Sanke shrugged.

"I don't know. She mostly just sulks in her room."

"Well," Catherine said with a warm smile, "maybe she'll perk up once we get to the preserve."

She rubbed Sanke on the back as they returned to their singing.

CHAPTER 6

That evening in the castle, a pair of guards slowly made their way up one of the many winding corridors. There was nothing particularly unique about it to set it apart from any other pathway in the place. The same architecture, same stone and pillars, same royal bunting spaced along the walls. The portion they patrolled wasn't in common use, so the lighting was a bit sparse this time of night, but apart from that it could have been mistaken for any other place on the premises.

Once they'd passed, a patch of stone on the wall, set deep in shadow, silently slid away.

Jenneca crawled from the opening and checked to make sure the hall was clear before slinking off into the night.

BOOK 7: DISMISSED
PART 2

CHAPTER 1

Jenneca's cabin aboard the royal cruiser lay empty. Not even light inhabited the space. Her carry-on bag sat on a stand next to the bed, untouched since it had been placed there hours earlier.

A knock came upon the door.

"Jenn. Honey? We're going to be setting down in about twenty minutes. The chefs want to know what you want for supper. Jenn?"

Catherine Hammond stood in the hallway outside the state room awaiting a response.

Sanke approached her from further down the cleanly illuminated corridor.

"What's good?" she asked.

"Jenneca won't answer me."

"Do you think she's in the tub? Or has her headphones on?"

"I don't know." Catherine pounded the door again. "Jenneca!"

"Here." Sanke tapped a small reflective plate embedded in the doorjamb. Even out in the hallway they could hear the loud chime it elicited within the room. "She must've heard that. It'd even interrupt her audio."

Catherine pressed the plate again. "Why isn't she..."

Sanke went for the door mechanism, located just beneath the call button. She'd barely touched it when the door effortlessly rolled open.

She and Catherine shared a confused look before peeking into the room.

"Jenneca, are you decent?" Catherine asked.

Each of them scanned the empty space. Though it was a sizeable cabin, the layout was fairly plain, with few places to hide from view. Sanke even swung herself around the doorframe to glance into the unlit lavatory. It only took a matter of seconds for them to conclude there was no occupant within.

Their eyes met again as the furrow of their brows deepened and their jaws clenched.

Back on the throne world, Jenneca silently treaded through the shadows of the palace, making her way towards the Tower of Justice.

The trekking was easy. Having lived there her whole life she easily knew the comings and goings, the rounds of the palace guard. She knew the feel and the sounds of the place so that she could deftly avoided any patrols or errant attendants.

Until she rounded one corner and found Neva headed towards her.

"There you are," Neva said.

"Gah!" Jenneca hopped back, momentarily losing control of her stealth practices. "Shh. Are you trying to get me caught? What're you doing here, anyway?"

"I saw you sneaking off the ship."

"Yeah, because I'm the impulsive one. Don't steal my thing."

"Impulsive, or irresponsible?" Neva asked.

"I am being responsible," Jenneca said. "All I ever did growing up was be responsible."

"Okay." Awkward silence filled the already-quiet hall. "I don't want the Crown, you know."

"This isn't about... I don't have a say in the matter, okay?

It can't go to me. That's not the point. My mom's not letting me help because she's overprotective."

"She lets you play with tanks for fun," Neva reminded her.

"Yeah, but… it's hard to explain, and I'm not really going to try right now. I need to get moving before I'm caught."

"You're going to go talk to Naoke… er, Angela, aren't you?" Neva asked.

"Yeah. And since you're here, for some reason, you should probably come along."

Neva made no remark before Jenneca was off down the hall. She of course followed along.

CHAPTER 2

The next morning at the Ao Sea, a small contingent of Kaian vessels moved stealthily through the water, some distance from the assembling Palan fleet.

Val and Bontu stood at the bow of one of the ships. Being on a maritime military action, Val was allowed to wear a royal uniform. That meant she could eschew the normally-required gowns, skirts, and dresses of her station in favor of her beloved trousers.

Their boat was unassuming; nothing about it stood out from the rest of the fleet. Nothing marked it as more important than any other; certainly nothing indicated that it was carrying royalty.

"You think they know we're here?" Bontu asked.

"I don't know," Val replied. "They're Palans. Their intelligence apparatus is a bit creaky. I actually had an even easier time hacking into their comms system than I thought I would."

Bontu held an ocular scope up to his eye and pointed it towards the towering Palan ships. Having completed interlocking a layer of them, the ships had begun landing atop one another, connecting top to bottom as well as side to side.

"Why do you think they're stacking them like that?" he asked.

Val took the scope from him and peered in the Palans' direction. She took a few moments to study the landing pattern.

"Oh, goddammit."

"What?" asked Bontu.

"They're making a palace."

"How can you tell?"

"The support structure is similar to the palace ship," Val lowered the scope and gestured out across the water. "They're building their own palace out of warships. On the other side of the planet from us."

"It does send a message, I suppose."

"They just need a monarch to put in it."

Back in her cell, Angela was lying on the bench, lazily tossing a rock into the air and catching it with one hand. Again and again. And again. Over and over.

A pair of slight silhouettes emerged from the hallway and worked their way into the room.

"Oh. You're here." Angela caught the rock one last time and sat herself up to meet them.

"Yeah," said Jenneca.

"I'll keep a lookout," said Neva.

She went to the door, her back to the cell. Jenneca faced Angela. Even with the bars between them, something in the core of her shook.

"And what do you want?" Angela asked.

"I want to talk to you."

"Let me guess, about your mother."

"Yeah."

"She is the last thing I want to talk about right now." Angela looked around. Then down at the rock in her hand. "But, as I've no other forms of real entertainment currently..."

She tossed the bit of rubble aside and dusted her hands before spreading her arms wide.

"Well," she said. "Say what you came to say."

"What do you have against my mother?" Jenneca asked.

Angela blurted out a laugh.

"Is that a serious question?"

"Yes." Jenneca inched forward. "I know she killed your father, but that was war. A war he started."

"Were you there?" Angela asked. Jenneca glared at her. "You know how they say that history is written by the winners? Your mom won that war. Whether she was right or wrong morally, she was 'right' in the eyes of history. But you're only hearing one side of things."

"Maybe," Jenneca acknowledged. "Did it never occur to you that the side you're hearing might be just as skewed, if not more so?"

"What does it matter? We are where destiny has placed us."

"But you don't have to be."

Angela broke eye contact to glance at the bars in front of her.

"My mother said something very similar. Suppose I decided not to be here. Suppose I just activate the Crown, pull these bars from their mortar, and slay you where you stand."

"Please don't do that."

"You don't want to die?" Angela asked.

"No."

"Did you not think it was a distinct possibility when you came here?"

"I just came to talk," Jenneca said.

"And are you naïve enough to think I mightn't pose a danger?"

"I wouldn't say naïve. Hopeful, maybe?"

Angela laughed again.

"Your laugh is really unsettling," Jenneca told her.

"Well, lucky for you, your optimism paid off. My quarrel is with your mother, not you. I won't hold you responsible for her actions, especially ones that predate your birth."

"Gee, thanks."

"But I will have what is mine." Angela rose up from her

seat and stepped towards the bars. "I will have the throne of Kaia, one way or another. If that means I have to go through your mother to get it, then that is what it shall be."

"You think so little of my mother," said Jenneca. "Why do you think she hasn't killed you already?"

"She can't." Angela touched the crown on her forehead. "Not while I have this."

"But you didn't have that until a day or two ago. Before that..."

"Before that she didn't know me or the threat I represent."

"There were a couple days there where..."

"Where she had me caged, but I didn't have the Crown," said Angela. "She underestimated me."

Jenneca worked to prevent her lip from curling into a sneer.

"See what happens if she ever gets you at her mercy again."

"She won't. I'll make sure of it. I will never be at her, or anyone else's, mercy ever again."

"Just wait," said Jenneca. "You'll see."

"We will, won't we?"

Jenneca glowered as she headed back for the doorway, grabbing Neva's arm and pulling her from the room.

Angela gave a small wave. "Feel free to stop by again, anytime!" She looked around. "Now, where'd my stone go?"

Neva and Jenneca hurried from the holding area before the next patrol came.

"Now what?" Neva asked.

Jenneca failed to look in her direction.

"I may not have planned that far."

CHAPTER 3

One thing about travel by water was that it was definitely slower than by air.

Val leaned against the deck rail, watching the crew of the ship go about their tasks.

Not everyone aboard, though, was part of the crew. Aside from those working the ship there were several contingents of maritime soldiers on standby.

"Anybody know any good show tunes?"

The soldiers looked between themselves. Few were quite sure that their queen was directly addressing them, but all were taken aback by the question.

One brave lad took a breath. His voice trembled as the words slowly spilled from his lips. His eyes found a spot on the deck and fixated there.

"Can I call on you?

"If ever you need me just call me and I will be there.

"I'll fight by your side."

He looked to find Val staring at him.

"Sorry, your highness." He lowered his gaze again.

Val smiled. "No, keep going. It's one of my favorites. You're butchering the hell out of it, but still."

As he continued on with the chorus, others gradually joined in.

"Can we call on the queen?

"If ever you need me just call me and I will be there.

"I'll save your life."

They began to stomp in rhythm.

"Hoo. Ah. Hoo. Ah. Hoo. Ah."

The singing trailed off as Bontu approached, carrying a pair of steaming mugs. He handed one to Val.

"Here. It's cold out here. Those guys caterwauling won't keep you warm."

"They were being nice." Val looked at the cup in her hands. "Who made it?"

"I did."

"Alright."

She took a sip.

Bontu joined her against the rail.

"So, how're things?" he asked.

"In general, or…?"

"With regards to the Palan situation," he said. "Let's limit it to that for now."

Her chin nodded towards the Palan construction zone off the shore.

"So far they're just building. They haven't made any aggressive moves."

"Other than actually being here."

"Well, there's that. Yeah. We keep circling, they keep landing ships. We're at something of an impasse."

"How much longer do we have to tolerate them violating our world?" Bontu asked.

"I'm not sure. I really want to avoid an incident. The type that leads to galactic war, I mean. I've seen more than enough of that. I don't really have a taste for any more."

"I know what you mean." His voice was weighty. "My axe is always yours, but it's gotten heavier as the years have worn on."

"Yeah, but we…" Her peripheral vision caught something in the sky. "Hang on. You still have that scope?"

Bontu turned to the crew.

"Someone get the queen a scope."

One of the crew members rushed over, tugging the cylindrical device loose from his belt and holding it towards them. Bontu took it and passed it over to Val. She held it to her eye and lifted her view skyward.

"What do you see?" Bontu asked.

Val lowered the scope to her side.

"Vaguely? Trouble."

"And not-so-vaguely," Bontu said.

"The Palan palace ship."

"The plancin… Palan plalace… palace ship," Bontu said. "I didn't even know they had one of those."

"They didn't, until recently," Val said. "They totally copied us, by the way."

"If they had one of those, why even bother constructing one out of warships?"

"Because their palace ship is tiny and fairly unimpressive. On its own it's basically a funny-shaped cruiser. I guess this was their plan for it all along."

"Hm." Bontu grunted. "Not a great plan."

"It's working, isn't it?"

"Only because you're being exceedingly patient," he said.

"Maybe he was counting on that." She drummed a pattern against her leg. "Have the captain narrow our circling distance by a hundred meters, see how they react."

Bontu nodded and headed off. It took little time at all for him to return, and by the time he had the boat had already changed course, angling in towards the makeshift Palan structure.

The sea craft continued on that way for a few minutes. As they circled around, the hangar on one of the warships opened. A squadron of fighters was expelled towards the naval vessels.

The aircraft quickly matched pace with the boats. A series of shots was blasted into the water just off the port side of the Kaian flotilla.

Displaced water from the detonations showered Val and Bontu and sloshed across the deck.

"Oh, they don't like that at all," said Val.

"Those were warning shots," said Bontu.

"Consider us warned."

The captain looked over to them from the helm position.

"Orders, your highness?" he asked.

"Take us closer. I would have words with Domnock."

Bontu and the captain shared a worried glance but the captain did as he was told.

The ship careened towards the Palan settlement. Its companion vessels did likewise.

The Palan flyers let off another round of fire on the port side.

"Getting a touch close there," Val said.

"What now?" asked Bontu.

"I'm not going to be warned off on my planet. Scorch their skins. Don't go for a direct hit."

Bontu smiled and headed for the nearest gunner station.

The boat fired up towards the Palan aircraft, only just missing them.

"Your highness," the captain called, "we're receiving a comm from the Palan fighters."

"I thought we might."

Val left her perch on the railing and headed into the communication room.

"Put it through," she said to the comm officer once she'd squeezed herself into the cramped office.

"Audio only, your highness." The comm officer worked the sliders of the control board.

"That's fine."

Life crackled into the audio equipment.

"Attention Kaian craft: desist in your current attack and move away from the palace ship. This will be your only warning."

Val took the microphone from the console.

"Palan craft, this is Queen Valentina. We will not be told where we may place our vessels on our own planet. Break off pursuit or we will have no choice but to declare your current course of action as an act of war. I don't think anyone wants that."

Only a low background hiss came from the receiver.

"They can hear me, right?" Val asked the comm officer.

The radio crackled in again.

"Kaian craft, we have received your message. Please be advised that our Kaian allies have informed us that you are enemies of the state and that you will be treated as such."

"Well that's not good."

The deck pitched below her as the boat was rocked by fire from the Palans.

"Contact our perimeter ships," Val told the comm officer. "Get us some air support."

"Aye."

Val rushed back out to the main deck.

There she found the boat's guns lit, peppering the air with fire. At least a few fighter craft were already missing from the previous formation.

Plasma fire continued to rain down from the aircraft. More of the warships were opening, threatening to release further attackers.

"Is this what you were planning?" Bontu hollered over the roar of the battle.

"To be honest, I was kind of hoping they'd back down. But I knew this was a possibility."

The comm officer came running from the ship's innards. There was something distressed about his appearance, and not just from the heaving of the boat beneath him that made his every step fraught and unsteady.

The entire ship shuddered, sending numerous crewmen sprawling, including the comm officer. Undeterred in his duty, he crawled towards Val until he could get his feet under him again.

She moved to help him up.

"What's going on?" she asked.

"My queen, I…"

The ship was rocked again, hard, sending sailors flying.

Val herself was thrown to the deck and drenched in spraying sea water.

"Are our shields even up?!" she asked the captain.

"Yes, your highness."

"We just need to hold out until the air support gets here," she told him.

"That's what I came to tell you," the comm officer said. "The air support's not coming."

"What?" Val balked. "Tell the generals they don't have a say in it. I'm ordering them to deploy, now."

"I know. I'm sorry. General Kendall is saying he won't recognize an order from you."

"Oh, shit. Don't tell me."

"He's recognizing Queen Angela as his commander-in-chief."

"Goddammit."

The ship was jolted again.

Among the chaos, Val found Bontu. She tried screaming to him, but it was swallowed by the increasing chaos of the situation.

The boat was thrown up, rising nearly perpendicular to the water, before slamming back down.

Bontu rubbed the salty water from his eyes and looked around the deck.

"Do we have new orders?" the captain asked.

"Where's Val?" Bontu replied.

The captain and crew quickly surveyed the open deck. Their queen was nowhere to be seen.

"If she's unavailable to discharge her duties, command would fall to you, guardian."

Bontu growled. "Alright, pull us out of here. This was an act of war, but until we know exactly what's going on, we're not in a strong position to wage it."

CHAPTER 4

Within a hidden compartment in the castle walls, Neva sat curled. She couldn't quite tell how large the space was, but she figured not very. It was surprisingly clean, likely owed to seldom being seen, touched, or accessed in any way by anyone or anything.

Giving her some clue as to the dimensions of the area was that Jenneca crouched as she approached. She carried with her a lantern in one hand, the other cradled to hold a loaf of fresh bread and various other foodstuffs.

"I'm back," she announced. "Dinner is served."

Jenneca nestled her lantern to her shoulder so that the two of them could see what they were eating.

"Jeez," said Neva.

"What?"

"This stuff is good."

"It is?" Jenneca asked.

"Yeah. You don't think so?"

"I don't know. I guess. I mean, it's just stuff I grabbed from the kitchen when no one was looking. It's not like I could ask any of the chefs to make us anything when we're supposed to be off-world."

"Okay, yeah. That's true. Maybe..." Neva cut herself short.

"What?"

"Maybe you're just so used to it that you don't even realize anymore how good it is."

"Oh, jeez," Jenneca said between bites. "Am I spoiled?"

"You're literally a princess," Neva replied.

"Okay, sure, but I've always sort of thought of myself as pretty grounded."

Neva's head instinctively pulled back, placing her pupils at the very corners of her eyes as she looked at her compatriot.

"For a princess," Jenneca added.

Neva shrugged and returned her attention to their meal.

"What did you think of me?" Jenneca asked.

"What?"

"Before. Before you knew who you were. When you were..." Jenneca gestured outward, almost dropping the lantern. She quickly caught it and secured it once more between her cheek and shoulder. "Out there."

"I... to be honest, I didn't really think about you much."

"You didn't think about me much, or didn't think much of me?"

"The first one. Which is what I said. I have... had a life. I had school and work and family and friends. I didn't have much room in my schedule to worry about the people who lived in a literal castle hundreds of miles away."

"Oh," Jenneca peeped.

"Are you disappointed?"

"No."

"You sound disappointed."

"Why would I be disappointed?"

"I don't know. You just sounded like you are."

"Well I'm not."

"Okay."

"I mean, I am – or was – the heir to the throne. My birthday is a national holiday. I would have thought that people thought of me."

"I'm sure some people do. Just not me."

"Okay. So you think you're better than other people?" Jenneca asked.

"What the hell? Where is that coming from?"

"You think because you don't spend time worrying about 'those silly royals' that you're superior to people who do care how their empire's being run?"

"That is not what I said at all," said Neva. "I think you're projecting. Or something. I don't know."

"No."

"If you say so."

"Maybe. I don't know. Ever since I found out... about us... I've just been trying not to think about it. But I should have had the life you had, and you should have had mine. You should be heir apparent to the throne."

"I still might be," said Neva.

"Whatever. And I should have had to have school and a job and those should be my family and friends."

"Yes to the family, but it's not like we would have had identical lives if we hadn't been switched. We're two different people."

"And instead I grew up in the castle, waited on night and day, eating food I don't even appreciate."

She took the lantern from her shoulder and smacked it down on the floor before turning away.

Neva sat awkwardly in the dim light.

"Um, so... are we staying here, or is there somewhere else we should go?" she asked. "When we're done eating."

"I don't know," Jenneca said. "These tunnels run through the whole castle. My mom could walk them all blindfolded, but she doesn't know we're here, hopefully, so she won't think to look."

"Why would she need to be blindfolded?" Neva asked. "She could just not bring a lantern. Wouldn't that have the same effect?"

"Shut up."

"Okay."

Neva tried to eat quieter.

◆ ◆ ◆

At the base of the makeshift Palan palace craft, unseen by any eyes, Val rose from the water in full armor. She pulled herself up and into an airlock and sealed it behind her.

Guards escorted Kavana and Clerak into the throne room atop that very structure. There they found, sat upon the throne, Kavana's brother; his wife occupied the chair just next to him.

"My liege, these two say they have business with you," said one of the guards.

Domnock smiled and descended from his pedestal.

"Of course. Do you not recognize my wayward sister?"

Domnock pulled Kavana towards him, wrapping her in a hardy embrace.

"Hello, Domnock," she said.

"And her lovely wife." Domnock moved to hug Clerak.

"I'm not much of a hugger." Clerak kept her hands folded in front of her.

"But my brother is," said Kavana.

Domnock smiled as he threw his arms around Clerak. She could only grin and bear it until finally, finally he released her.

"Okay, that's quite enough," she said.

"And meet my own beloved." Domnock turned and gestured to his wife with a toothy beam of pride.

The Palan queen smiled and waved to them, never once making a move to rise from her seat.

"Hello, dear sister," she said.

Kavana and Clerak nodded to her.

Domnock swung an arm out towards the tables of food and drink.

"Please, join me," he said.

Kavana went to one of the buffets to pick at a tray of still-steaming meat products.

"Hm, quite the indulgent spread," she said.

"That's how father stayed so hearty all those years,"

Domnock replied.

"That's one way of putting it," his sister said.

"I'll also remind you that my coronation celebration had to be cut short to rush to your aid."

"For which I am eternally grateful."

"And for which I am eternally hungry." He grabbed a slab of meat from beneath her hand and stuffed it into his face. "Mm. Tender."

"It better be," his wife said. "You left it warming for three days."

"These things can take a week or more to fully cook," said Domnock. "Luckily our chefs are the most talented in the known kingdoms."

Kavana picked up a plate and began filling it.

"It's been so long since I've enjoyed real Palan food," she said.

"You never told me that you missed it," said Clerak.

"Because I know you'd try to make some sort of gesture out of it. No offense, dear, you're a fine cook, but nothing compares to the flavors a true Palan chef imbues their work with."

Clerak picked a piece of something off her plate and shoved it into her mouth.

She shrugged.

"It's alright."

"Alright?" Domnock balked.

"Forgive Clerak, please," Kavana urged. "Her palette wasn't raised on Palan fine dining."

"Food in the Kaian palace was more than adequate," Clerak said.

"Now now, let's not turn this into a competition, dear. Here." She filled a glass and handed it to Clerak. "Have some wine."

"I don't typically drink wine," Clerak said.

"But we're celebrating today," Kavana said.

"And what are we celebrating?" Clerak asked.

Kavana smiled as she turned to her brother and tipped her own glass.

"Why, a family reunion, of course."

CHAPTER 5

The captain sloshed his way across the deck of the Kaian flagship towards Bontu, who now stood at the bow himself, observing the Palan palace structure in the distance.

The deck itself was still something of a frightful sight, besieged by flooding and the scorched markings of battle.

"Sir," said the captain, "we still cannot find the queen anywhere aboard."

"Well of course you can't." Bontu nodded towards the makeshift palace. "She's on the Palan ship."

At that same moment, Val stalked the hallways of the Palan complex, shrugging off gunfire from retreating soldiers as she moved through its corridors.

She lunged at one of them, gripping the barrel of his firearm and forcing it away from herself.

"Do you ever even think about the poor soul whose job it is to sweep up all these bullet casings you're needlessly scattering all over the place? No, you only think about yourself."

She crumpled the rifle in her hand and tossed it aside, then gave the soldier a shove, sending him flailing back into his compatriots.

Past the pile of ineffectual sentries, she continued onward.

◆ ◆ ◆

It was just a few moments later, within the throne room, that Domnock and the others heard the commotion from outside.

"What is going on out there?" Domnock demanded.

Threw the opened doorway, a trio of soldiers were launched into the room; Val followed closely behind.

She took a moment to survey the area.

"Oh, good, you're all here. That's very considerate of you. Saves me a lot of time."

Kavana stood frozen in place, her fingertips pressing hard against the plate still gripped in her hand.

Clerak grabbed a gun from the nearest guard and took aim at Val.

She quickly lowered the weapon again.

"Sorry. Force of habit."

She tossed the gun to the ground. It clattered to a stop at Val's feet.

"Glad to see at least one of you has some sense," said Val.

Kavana leaned in to Clerak.

"Gee, maybe if we hadn't left a certain someone back in her cell this wouldn't seem like such a major catastrophe."

"We'll be fine," said Domnock.

"That depends," said Val. "If you pack up your stuff and get the hell off my planet in the next, say, two hours, you'll be okay. If you don't, we're going to have problems."

"It's not your planet anymore," said Clerak. "I'm sure you've felt it slipping away from you in recent days. I couldn't help but notice a lack of air support for you earlier. How's General Kendall doing these days?"

"I feel I'm being very generous by giving you the two hours." She pointed to Kavana and Clerak. "Though you two are going back to jail."

"Surely you can't be serious," said Kavana. "We're the

mothers of the queen."

Val stepped towards them. She was stopped as the air around her buzzed. Domnock had scurried to the throne, his fingers pressing a hidden control in the armrest.

"A force field? Huh."

Val reached out and pushed against the energy barrier. It illuminated where she made contact. She slowly walked forward, straining and stretching the field.

"Is it supposed to be doing that?" Kavana asked.

"My dear sister, I will see you in a bit." Domnock threw himself onto the throne and hit another control. An energy dome encased him before the entire setup dropped into the floor. His wife's seat did the same.

"Seriously?" Val asked. "An ejector throne? Who even thinks of that?"

She looked to the others still remaining as she continued her advance.

"He just left us?" Clerak asked.

"Of course, darling," said Kavana. "Family is everything, but oneself is always the priority."

"Hey, how long you figure before I make it through?" Val asked. "Like, seconds? Minutes?"

She heard the projector mechanism creak.

"Probably seconds."

Kavana and Clerak pivoted and sprinted for the far exit.

Val heard another buzz behind her: a second field activating.

There came another sound, a short click.

"Ah, crap."

Fire engulfed her.

Not just her, but a good portion of that level of the ship.

The explosion near the top of the palace structure threw Val clear, sending her hurtling far down to the water below.

CHAPTER 6

T he auxiliary throne room, to which Domnock and his wife safely made it, was not as large as the original, and the thrones sat at ground level there. Nor was it adorned with the celebratory feast; Domnock and his wife had managed to secure a few plates and goblets for themselves before making their escape.

"They've, um, headed elsewhere, I presume," Domnock could be heard saying to his wife as a young woman unexpectedly entered. Horrified expressions came over the pair of them at the sight of her. "Who're... do we have any level of security in any of the throne rooms?"

Guards quickly rushed in from an adjoining chamber to surround the new arrival.

"Surely you don't mean to have me escorted out. Or worse." Her eyes briefly darted towards the guards as she advanced through the room. "You must know who I am."

Domnock motioned for the guards to halt.

He approached her and stood before her, towering above her. studying her face.

"Yes. I see your mother in you. And plenty of your father, as well."

Angela smiled.

"It's a kindness to finally meet you," he said.

"And you, uncle. Look at us now. Just a few days ago, neither of us were monarchs. Now..."

"Now we steer the fates of empires," he cackled. Angela nodded. "May I ask why I find you here?"

"My own palace is currently occupied," she said.

"Still? Then it truly is good that we've come here." Domnock swept his arms up. "All this is yours, dear niece. There's a bit of a mess to be cleaned upstairs, but otherwise you should find it satisfactory."

"It is always good to receive family, but not like this," she said.

He looked down his nose at her.

"How do you mean?"

"Hold your forces in ready. Do not move against the false queen."

"I can only maintain a holding pattern for so long, my dear. There was already a, ah, bit of a skirmish earlier."

"I'm asking you to hold it just a bit longer."

"Why?"

"Because it's not needed, and if all goes well it never will be."

Domnock's face flared.

"Not needed? Do you have any idea what lengths I had to go to to bring this force to Kaia."

"My mother has made me very aware of all the maneuvers, yes."

"I did this for your mother's sake."

"I am not my mother. I don't need her, or you, or anyone else to fight my battles for me."

"What are you suggesting, little one?"

"What I am telling you, dear uncle, is that I will handle my cousin myself."

BOOK 8: DISMISSED
PART 3

CHAPTER 1

The water along the rocky shore of the Ao Sea broke, heralding the exit of the Queen of Kaia.

Val pulled herself from its black grip and, liquid still pouring from every crevasse of her enchanted armor, dragged herself onto the coastline.

Once on her feet, she stood motionless, waiting for the salty water to finish flowing off her body.

Remaining planted, she was rapidly approached by a contingent of soldiers led by her oversized cousin.

"Val! Are you alright?" Bontu asked.

"Yeah. Just letting the armor drip-dry. Otherwise when I take it off my clothes get soaked."

"But you're alright otherwise?"

"Yeah. Though the look on your face tells me I might not be for long."

"We've received word from the palace." What could be seen of Bontu's face was stern, more so than Val was used to. "It's a bloodbath there."

"What?!"

"General Kendall's forces, those loyal to Angelo and his daughter, they're trying to take the place by force. So far defenses have held, but there are attacks coming from within."

"No." Val's voice was sharp, pointed. "This is not happening. The palace does not fall under my watch. And yes, I remember the business with the Artondy. Totally different. Do you have transport to Olivert?"

"Ready and awaiting."

Val followed him a short distance away to a waiting airship.

They quickly ascended the side ramp into the vessel.

"Ah, see, it's getting all over the carpet."

CHAPTER 2

The defensive force fields around the castle were peppered with rippling energy impacts. Warships hovered nearby. Some launched their cannon fire towards the castle; others fired on those assaulting the capitol. All bore the colors of Kaia.

The transport ship carrying Val and Bontu approached mostly unimpeded, barely having to weave through the hail of plasma fire.

"Drop me off at the front gate." Val stood behind the pilot in the cockpit.

"I'm sorry, my queen, it's not safe to approach from that side. Our ships have cleared us a path to the rear landing platform."

"It's probably better that way," Bontu said. "Now's not the time to go jumping straight into battle."

"But I really want to bust something up for attacking my home," said Val. "Probably a character flaw of mine."

"Have we a status update from the palace?" Bontu asked.

"Shields are currently around fifty-eight percent." The co-pilot read from a screen, keeping one eye on their flight path. "No worries about a breach for now. But ground fighting is producing a lot of casualties. No reports on numbers just yet."

"This is unacceptable," said Val. "They do not do this in my house."

"Understood, ma'am," said the co-pilot. "We're getting you

home just as fast as possible."

Val paced the cockpit floor, her boot steps eliciting a steady pattern of sharp, metallic clangs. Bontu looked away and focused his gaze out the front viewport.

The ship swung around to the back of the castle and approached the circular landing platform at its rear.

"Syncing shield harmonics now," the pilot announced as he worked the ship's control console. "We just have to hope the insurgents didn't do anything to them."

"Wait, is that an actual concern?" Bontu asked.

The transport ship glided through the shield and came to a landing.

The pilot let out a small breath and smiled.

"See, nothing to worry about."

"Then why'd you even bring it up?" Bontu asked.

He turned around to find Val already gone.

As the side hatch of the transport opened, Val didn't wait for it to finish extending before hopping down and making for the catwalk to the castle. She was already armored up and ready for action.

Gunfire sprayed the path in front of her. A few soldiers hid near the other end of the walkway, guns drawn. Experience had taught her that for every one she could see there would be several more that she couldn't.

"That's far enough," one of the soldiers called to her. "Please, my q... please don't make this any harder than it has to be."

She continued towards them.

"Don't presume to tell me what to do in my own home. I've fought beside most of you. You know what I'm capable of. I don't want anyone hurt, but given the circumstances, I'm not sure I can manage to be gentle enough to seem merciful."

The gunfire continued. She ignored it and trudged on.

A pair of soldiers appeared in the doorway. One slammed a tripod to the ground, the other hastily set a bulky, silvery device atop it: a proton cannon.

The full contraction stood more than waist-height on either of them. The cannon was nearly as long as they were tall, with a pair of hand-grips rigged to one end.

"Ah, shit." Val dove to one side as the cannon was fired. An impossibly wide stream of energy with a white-hot core shot forth.

The kickback on the cannon was strong. Under ordinary circumstances, it was used as an anti-vehicle armament and would usually be found attached to a mobile weapons platform.

The gunners operating it struggled to keep it properly aimed. Though, with a firing field as wide as it was, precision was neither particularly possible nor necessary.

The stone and mortar catwalk took a good deal of the brunt of the blasting; chunks were torn out of it and sent spraying high into the air with each volley. Visibility was cut drastically by the fog of detritus that hung in the air.

After several bursts, each lasting a few seconds, the soldiers paused their firing.

Surveying the area, they found no trace of Val.

"Where is she? Where'd she go?"

"We didn't kill her, did we?"

"I don't know. Dammit. I mean, did we want to? I'm not sure..."

They caught sight of her again as she swung up from beneath the footbridge, catching the pair of them across their faces with the edge of her armored boots. The last of the soldiers in view, along with several hiding behind the door frame, opened fire at her with their automatic rifles. She was swiftly upon them, disarming the lot and knocking them clear from her path.

One of the discarded soldiers, somehow remaining conscious, managed to get to the cannon and spin it around. Only the distinct click of the trigger pull alerted Val to the danger.

"Jeez!"

Her enhanced reflexes allowed her to duck out of the way

and find a discarded firearm on the ground, while the armor's supernatural properties let her infuse it with crackling energy and throw it back towards her lone gunner. The charged weapon impacted the cannon along its length, breaching its shell and causing a reaction within the power cell at the gunner's end. The resulting explosion scorched the surrounding walls; the burned soldier was thrown clear out of the castle.

CHAPTER 3

The sounds of gunfire and screaming could be heard even through the thick stone walls that separated the main corridors of the palace from the hidden passage that Neva and Jenneca slunk through.

"We've been wandering for hours," Neva griped. "Where are we going?"

"Towards the communications office," Jenneca said. "Don't worry, we should be safe in here... HOLY HELL!"

The proton cannon burst that had moments earlier missed her mother tore through the walls of the passage directly in front of her. She stumbled back into Neva, who did her best to prop her upright.

"Okay back, back, back the other way." Jenneca's eyes were wide and her mouth dry.

They turned around and hurried back in the other direction.

The door to the throne room opened roughly on its ancient hinges, swinging as fast as it could towards the walls on either side of its frame. Not waiting for it to finish doing so, Val stormed her way in. The heavy boots of her armor elicited a metallic clang against the stone floors. She was not in a mood to attempt any sort of stealth.

Even with the enhancement to her vision afforded her by the Crown, she saw naught but an empty chamber.

"Dammit. Someone's got to be in charge around here. Where are they hiding themselves?"

"I'm not hiding from you."

Emerging from the deep shadows behind the throne at the top of the dais, Angela appeared to her in full armor.

"Goddammit are you thick," Val said. "Do you have any idea what you're doing? Do you have any idea what the sight of Kaians fighting Kaians is probably doing to the people? Most of them still remember the last civil war, the one your dad started. It cost thousands of lives and left scars that still aren't fully healed."

"Of course," Angela said as she descended the steps from the throne. "If they were healed, my mothers couldn't have exploited them."

"You're something else. I didn't want to have to hurt you. I really didn't. But you're not really leaving me any choice."

The two of them began circling one another, each taking the other's measure.

"You can't hurt me," Angela said. "My armor is stronger than yours."

"I suppose we'll see about that."

Angela moved to a ceremonial weapons rack against the wall. She raised up a dark sword, one nearly as long as the polearms beside it.

Val was quickly upon her.

"Oh, no, you don't get the ebonore one," she said, plucking the long black sword from the younger woman's grip.

"Fine." Angela took up a double-bladed battle axe and faced Val.

"You going to make the first move?"

"You've got the advantage in reach. I was waiting on you."

"That might not be the smartest idea."

Angela shrugged slightly.

Val swung the black blade at Angela, who deflected it

upward with the battle axe. Val swung again, a quick thrust across Angela's chest. It didn't leave much of a scratch.

Angela came at Val, catching the sword between the blade and handle of the axe and forcing it downward. She threw an elbow to Val's face; Val was staggered, giving Angela an opening to charge her axe with energy and spin, making a wide swing directly for Val's center mass.

Val found herself hurtled across the room. By the time she was able to regain her bearings, to say nothing of her footing, Angela had flung herself through the air, her axe ready again.

Val effortlessly rolled out of the way, allowing the axe to come down on the stone floor, blowing a large chunk out of it. In doing so, Val left her weapon sitting on the ground.

Rather than going for her sword, Val scooped up a handful of stone debris, charged it, and hurl it at Angela.

Angela had to pause her assault to shield her face from the impacts.

Val grabbed her sword, charged it, and swung it up, catching Angela between the armored plating on her left side. The sword barely cut into her, but it was enough to make the younger woman cry out in startled pain.

It took Val a moment to dislodge her weapon. When she had done so, Angela stumbled backwards. Ignoring the aching throb in her side, she stormed towards Val, her axe crackling with Crown energy. Val barely had time to charge up her own weapon and take a defensive stance before the two of them collided.

The resulting detonation sent the two of them tumbling out into the hallway.

The both of them scrambled to their feet and readied their weapons.

Angela came at Val, hacking and swinging. Val blocked and deflected the blows, but was unable to gain any momentum with which to go on the offensive. Instead, she was driven backwards, barely able to keep getting her blade up in time to stop her opponent's axe from crushing her.

Val continued backing up. Angela continued advancing.

They neared a stairwell with an open window. Val deflected one more swing from Angela before grabbing her and spinning for the aperture, sending them both tumbling out.

They spent little time in the air, the weight of their armor and the force of the jump speeding them towards the courtyard below. They impacted the ground hard. Both were slow getting up and gathering their weapons.

Val groaned. "This is getting ridiculous."

"Shame you didn't have a waiting ship this time, isn't it?" Angela asked.

"That would have been a good idea, yeah."

They squared off again.

Their blades smashed together, belting out a hideous knell into the darkened afternoon sky.

With additional room to maneuver her outsized sword, Val was more able to hold her own. Their blades collided again and again, ringing loudly enough to alert the soldiers fighting nearby.

All hostilities between the Kaian forces in the castle slowly ceased as they turned to see the excitement down below. Soldiers peered out of windows and huddled onto the catwalks to watch the two women do battle.

Their weapons clashed repeatedly, neither able to gain the upper hand for more than one or two blows.

Angela finally caught Val across the head with her axe, sending Val spiraling to the dirt.

Her hand probed for the point of impact and found a small crack in her helmet. She looked at her fingers and saw a smear of blood across them.

Val staggered to her feet just in time for Angela to throw a shoulder into her, knocking her back down.

Val rose as best she could, readying herself again, but found both of Angela's feet coming up towards her. The impact blasted her high into the air, clear over the castle's outer wall.

Val landed and tumbled for several meters, tearing up the

landscaping as she went, before managing to stop herself.

"Well, that was dumb," she said.

A mighty leap carried Angela over the wall after her. She landed nearby with a heavy impact.

"Yes, it was."

Val felt the side of her head. The crack in her armor was already healing and the bleeding seemed to have either stopped or been contained.

"I meant for you."

Val charged her sword and brought the tip down into the lawn. The already-cracked ground beneath Angela erupted, sending her twisting into the air amidst a torrent of earth and vegetation.

Before she could hit the ground again, Val was upon her, slashing at her with the charged ebonore blade. It wasn't until Angela hit the dirt again that she could mount a counterassault.

And assault she did, dropping her axe down into Val's left shoulder.

Val screamed out as she crumpled to the ground. A spray of blood had splashed across the golden visor of her helmet, limiting her vision on that side.

Undeterred, she lashed out with her sword, catching Angela between the legs before heaving on the blade. Angela flipped to the ground. The pair of them lay unmoving for several long, tense moments.

Val tried propping herself up, but the agony in her shoulder forced her back to the dirt. She rolled to her other side and tried again, barely able to rise to her knees.

Angela wasn't fairing much better. When Val had used the ebonore blade to trip her up, something was cut in the back of her leg. She could feel the mystical energies of the armor knitting the tissue back together, but for the moment her limb was useless.

Val grunted and groaned all the way to her feet. Seeing her opponent rise, Angela bore down, snarled through the pain, and pulled herself up.

The ebonore blade was a finely crafted weapon, but its size made it unwieldy without the power of the Crown armor to hoist it, and without two hands to guide it. With just the one good arm, Val dragged it along the ground as she approached Angela.

Though her mobility was limited by her still-healing leg, Angela was able to plant herself in place and swing her heavy axe, catching Val square in the chest and sending her back to the ground.

Val rose again.

Angela stumbled towards her and chopped again, pushing her back to the soil.

Val fought to catch her breath, but the pain from her shoulder made it a struggle. It wasn't healing as fast as she'd hoped and was slowing her every move.

She looked up to see Angela coming towards her again. Angela's leg no longer dragged as much.

Her injured arm was good for little more than propping the blade of her sword upon. She did so, raising the hilt with her good arm, hoping to produce enough of a barrier to Angela's axe to protect her vital areas.

She sat there, waiting for the strike to come.

Then she heard a loud bang in the distance. Then another. They came in a rhythm. More joined in, a choir of makeshift drumming.

Val looked around to find the soldiers, previously silent onlookers, encircling the walls, kneeling, banging the butts of their rifles against the stone embankments of the castle.

Then voices started in.

"Hoo. AH! Hoo. AH! Hoo. AH!"

Beneath her mask, Val smiled.

She spun around, charging her sword, and struck Angela square across the midsection. Angela was sent sprawling to the ground, losing control of her axe.

Val ran at her. A lifetime of training taught her not to launch herself into the air. Whatever advantage that might give her in speed would be lost in control.

Val shoved her sword blade into the air and brought it down at Angela.

The blade was caught between Angela's palms.

Angela was startled to see the ebonore crackle with energy. Before she could do anything, the energy detonated. She yelped as the explosion burned her palms, but did not relent.

Val braced her hand at the pommel of the hilt and pushed harder, forcing it towards Angela's face.

Angela bore down, focused, and shoved back, forcing Val away again.

Before either combatant could resume their attack, plasma fire rained down from above, blasting the ground between the two of them.

Val was sent skittering towards the edge of the abyss that surrounded the castle. She managed to work up enough momentum to throw herself over the yawning chasm, rolling to safety on the other side.

Angela was thrown back into the castle wall.

She looked up to find a Palan warship firing towards Val. Several more ships of the same design were descending from the sky.

"No, you idiots!" Angela shouted.

Val dashed between the onslaught from the warship. The pain in her shoulder was only just starting to relent, but her legs worked as well as ever.

Angela tapped the side of her helmet.

"Mum, are you there?"

"We're here for you," came Clerak's voice in her ear.

"No, call off the attack," Angela said. "I can do this."

"Are you sure?"

"Yes! Do you have any idea how bad it looks to have a Palan ship attacking the palace?"

"Your mother convinced Domnock to build you a new palace."

"Please just do as I ask," said Angela.

"Alright. I hope you don't regret this."

The Palan ships halted their fire and pulled up, their shadows across the castle lessening.

Angela ran and leapt over the abyss, landing gracefully on the other side.

Val gripped her sword and stood ready.

"Forget something?" she asked.

"I don't need it."

Angela's fists ignited as she advanced on her opponent.

Val lashed out with her sword. Angela used nothing but her forearms to block and deflect the strokes.

Her fist made it through, catching Val solidly in the stomach. Val was staggered, the wind suddenly forced from her lungs. While Val clutched at her chest, desperate for air, Angela grabbed the spikes of her crown and brought her face down into her knee. Angela hopped into the air and brought her forearm down on Val's back, sending a shockwave of pain through her body.

Val lay on the ground, waiting for the Crown to heal her enough to be able to move again. It only took a few moments, but that was all the time it took for Angela to lift her off the ground and punt her across the nearby field. Her ebonore sword was left behind.

"Okay." Val had gotten herself to her feet by the time Angela was upon her again.

Angela came at her swinging the ebonore blade. Val blocked the first swipe with her forearm, then the next. Both left gouges in her armor.

On the third, she was able to grab Angela's arm and flip her around, slamming her down on her back.

The sword was sent spinning into the air. Val grabbed it and brought it down, flowing with energy, through Angela's shoulder. The younger girl tried to move but the blade had gone straight through and into the terrain beneath her. She was pinned down and screaming in agony.

"Do you yield?" Val asked.

Angela continued thrashing and shrieking, unable to work herself free.

"Do you yield?" Val repeated. "I need an answer."

"N—n–n…"

"Please… please yield."

Angela did her best to compose herself. "I don't want to die."

"You won't, if you stand down."

Still whimpering, Angela was able to haltingly turn her head to have a look at her shoulder. Blood seeped from around the sword blade on both sides of the wound.

"We can get you to the med bay, you'll be fine," Val said. "But you need to give up. Now."

Slowly, Angela nodded.

Val stood.

"I'm trusting you," she said. "I hope you realize what a big leap of faith that is."

Angela reached up with her free arm and pried up the Crown. Her armor retracted into it, leaving her exposed.

The energy pumping through the sword dissipated and Val pulled it from Angela's shoulder.

"You fought well," Val said. "There's no shame in defeat."

Tears flowed freely from Angela's eyes.

Val looked at the bleeding wound. "I know, it hurts, but you're going to be alright."

Val tore a section of Angela's tunic away and wrapped it around the younger woman's lacerations.

"No I won't," Angela said. "I failed. My mothers are going to kill me."

"That won't happen. Whether you mean it literally or not. If your moms deserve to call themselves that, then they'd better love you no matter what."

Val was the first to hear the engine roar in the distance. Without the enhanced senses provided by the Crown, it was several moments before Angela caught up.

A Kaian tank rolled up.

The hatch popped open and Jenneca climbed out.

"Mom!"

"Jenneca? What the hell are you doing here?"

"Never mind that. The ships aren't stopping!"

"What?"

"I was just at the castle and overheard. The Palan ships are still attacking."

"It's my uncle," Angela said. "Mother said he was mad. And he hates you."

"Lots of people hate me, they don't all lay siege to our world about it."

Angela gripped the Crown of the Five Point Star. She held it out for Val.

"Here."

"What?" Jenneca asked.

Val placed a hand on Angela's. There was a spark of energy between the Crown and Val.

"Put it on," Val said. "We'll fight this together."

Angela shook her head.

"I'm in no shape to help." She pushed the Crown towards Val again. There was another jolt of energy. "Take it. Use it to defend our people."

Val gingerly took the Crown into her own hands.

"What about Neva?" Jenneca asked.

Neva poked her head out of the tank.

"What about me?" she asked.

"She's had almost no training. I can't ask her to go into combat." Val looked down at Angela. "You'll... still have to answer for what you've done."

"I know. I'll do it after Kaia is safe."

"And your mothers," Val said.

"I'll hunt them down myself, if I have to."

"You just might. They evaded me for your entire life and then some." Val hesitated. "Well, here goes this."

She lifted the Crown of the Five Point Star to her head. It trembled in her hands before leaping to her face. Val had nearly forgotten the rush of power that came with the addition of a new Crown, and this one was the mother of them all.

Her armor, so long stable, mutated one last time. The panels grew long, solid, more curved and anatomical. Lines of energy appeared across its surface. A pair of rings of pure illumination grew from her back. Bladed wings sprang forth from them.

In a streak of light, she was in the sky, rocketing away from the planet's surface. In just seconds, she was out of the atmosphere and barreling down on the war fleet that threatened her world.

Having not thought, in the burst of vitality the newly finished Crown brought, to bring a weapon, Val forged one out of pure energy, crafting a wide blade that extended from her arm.

She flew straight on, through the lead ship, and out the aft end.

The ship listed as it began to detonate from the inside out.

The other ships tried targeting her, but she was too small and fast. It was only a matter of seconds before the next ship was crippled.

Aboard one of the vessels, the crew rushed about the bridge, trying to defend themselves from Val, to destroy her if they could, not entirely certain what was going on.

Her voice came through, "Stand down. Leave Kaia, or be destroyed."

"That's not coming through the comm systems," the captain of the vessel said. "How the hell is she doing that?"

"What do we do, sir?" the first officer asked.

"Keep firing," the captain said. "It's only one... craft? Ship?"

The gunner crew looked at him, just as unsure of what they were targeting as he was.

They watched Val fly straight through another ship, sending it slowly pitching into its nearest sister. The hull from the damaged ship tore into the good, explosively decompressing the outer cabins.

"Whatever it is, sir, it's moving too fast for the systems to lock onto," the gunner said.

"Fire manually if you have to," said the captain.

"I'm trying sir, but... it's moving damn fast, and staying close to our vessels."

The captain collected himself. "Destruction of the target is the priority. Save our compatriots if you can, but take it out."

The gunner swallowed hard.

"Yes, sir."

Val fluttered between the ships, slashing along their hulls, punching through their shields.

Plasma fire trailed her, cutting its way through space, only stopping as it impacted other ships.

Val flew up in front of the lead spacecraft's bridge viewport.

The crew watched the strange figure hang there, bursting with light. She was too close to their own vessel for them to take aim at.

"Leave. Kaia."

"Uh... orders, sir?" the first officer asked.

Val floated in closer; she stabbed her energy blade into the viewport and slowly began slicing.

"Stand down," the captain ordered. "Stand down! Signal the rest of the fleet to do the same. We're leaving Kaia." He looked out the viewport. "Alright?"

Val pulled back.

A thick metal blast door slid down over the damaged viewport.

The Palan ships pulled away from the planet and began entering fold space.

CHAPTER 4

Val descended from the sky and gently came to a rest where she'd started, near the tank in the field. Jenneca and Neva were busy loading up the injured Angela.

"Mom," Jenneca paused, "that was... wow."

"Thanks. I do try."

"Yeah. I was, uh, just getting ready to take Angela back to the castle for treatment."

"Good. We should..." Val let out a stunned scream and dropped to her knees as the energy flowing through her flared. It moved across her like lightning and shot from her wings in sharp bolts.

Perhaps against all good sense, the three younger women rushed towards her.

"Mom!" yelled Jenneca.

"I... I'm understanding now," said Val.

"What?" Jenneca asked.

Val looked at her.

"Everything." Her body glowed more intensely. She turned towards the sky. "Oh, God, it's... everything has been leading to this. Kaia, the Order of Meridian, the Crowns, Andor's death, my mother whispering in my ear: you, Neva, Donnie, Angela. Kavana and the doctor. It's all connected. I..."

She looked at her hands. They were somehow beginning to lose physical cohesion, transforming into pure luminance.

"Oh, God. I can't stop it." She tried to stand but was

dropped back to her knees. "I can't stop."

"Mom," said Jenneca, "you're scaring me."

Val looked at her.

"Can I tell you a secret, hon? I'm scared, too."

Jenneca looked on helplessly as her mother doubled over, crying out in anguish. Her body began pulsing with light, phasing translucent with each flash.

"It's… getting hard… to think in words. My mind, it's like a stream of consciousness. There's too much…"

Angela ran in screaming.

"No!"

She lunged for Val, grabbing onto the Crown.

Jenneca tried to seize her but was kicked away.

Angela shrieked as the Crown burned the flesh from her fingers. Still, she did not relinquish her grasp.

"Angela." Val's voice sounded hollow, distant. "You still don't get it, do you? The re-forging of the Crown was defective. It gave you the power of the original, but none of the understanding. Lucky for you, I have understanding to spare."

Val placed a palm against Angela's forehead.

The light enveloped Angela. She cried out again and pulled back, finally letting the Crown slip from her hold.

Jenneca stood by.

"Mom. You can't go."

"I don't want to. I'm not sure I have a choice at this point."

"Please." Jenneca pleaded. "We still need you."

"I know. I'm sorry."

"No." Jenneca grabbed her mother's hand. "No!"

Angela stumbled away and fell to the ground.

Jenneca pulled, as if trying to drag her mother back from an unseen force that was attempting to carry her away.

But the force acting upon Valentina was not physical. Her body was not being pulled away so much as it was disappearing, transcending its material existence.

Still, Jenneca held fast.

"I still need you," she said.

With each pulse of light, Val noticed something. Her hand, and more and more of her arm, was not fading from sight.

"Jenneca."

"Mom?"

"Don't stop."

Val reached out, grabbing onto each of Jenneca's arms.

Angela got up, still woozy. Neva helped her. The two of them moved towards Jenneca and Val.

"I'll... I can help," Angela said.

"No!" Val kicked her away. As she crumpled to the dirt, Angela briefly glowed where she was kicked. She got up again.

Neva recoiled from the burning energy that danced through the air.

"Stay back," Val warned.

Neva grabbed onto Angela, stopping her in her tracks. Angela clung to Neva, wobbling a bit on her feet.

Val looked to Jenneca.

"Mom, I'm trying," Jenneca said. "You have to help me."

"I can't. I'm... sorry. I hope I prepared you for this."

Jenneca screamed. She released her hold on Val's arms, instead wrapping herself around her torso and flopping back.

They both cried out as they collapsed to the ground.

Val rolled off of her, the light fading from the Crown's armor.

Jenneca wheezed "Mom?"

Val cradled her face. "Thank you, honey. I'm so proud of you."

"Please call a medic," Jenneca said. "You landed on me and you're very heavy."

Val tapped her earpiece.

"This is the queen. Home in on my position..."

"We've got you, Val," came Bontu's voice over the radio. "We tracked you coming back down to Kaia. You weren't hard to spot."

"Medical, too?" Val asked.

"All the standard stuff."

"Thanks." She turned to Jenneca. "How bad is it?"

"I don't know. I hope not too bad."

"Does anything feel broken? Punctured?"

"I don't know."

"Where does it hurt?"

"Everywhere."

Angela cautiously approached.

"I understand now," she said. "I'm sorry."

"We'll worry about that later. I'm only concerned about my daughter's safety right now."

"I could have helped," Angela said. "I tried to help. You didn't have to do it alone."

Val pointed to Jenneca.

"She did, though. Anyone bound to the Crown, anyone of the blood, would just be pulled in, too. It had to be her. To bring me back. She was the only one."

CHAPTER 5

"I don't know what happens now," said Val.

"I'm fine just going home," Jenneca replied.

They sat in the back of a medical vehicle, tended to by field technicians. The landscape whizzed past the windows as they sped over the field and toward the castle.

"That's not what I meant," Val said. "I meant… long term. I don't know what happens. The Crown's been united. The universe has never seen anything like it. It's so powerful."

"So, do you have to get rid of it?"

"I don't think so. But I don't know. I hope not, but I can't say for sure. I just don't know what the future holds. Despite everything I saw when I had it on, I can't see the future. Is it too powerful now for one person to wear? If I put it on again, will what happened to me earlier happen again?"

"Don't put it on again," said Jenneca. "Please."

"I might have to someday. And it's not just me. If I can't contain it anymore, can anyone? Or is it lost to us now?"

Jenneca stared at her.

"I don't expect you to have the answers, sweetie," said Val.

"Good. Because I don't."

"And heading home sounds great about now."

Val took her daughter's hand, closed her eyes, and leaned back for the ride.

◆ ◆ ◆

Outside the castle, Val waited with a contingent of guards.

An armored transport, along with several escorts, approached up the road from the gates.

The transport came to a stop near the castle doors. A panel on the side split and opened. Kaian soldiers led Kavana and Clerak out.

"Clerak." Val folded her arms. "It's been a while."

"It should have been delayed indefinitely," said the former general.

"Sure. And Kavana. We've never really met before this week, have we? Amazing that you've spent nearly half your life hating someone you didn't even know."

"I don't need to know you for you to have ruined my life," said Kavana.

"You did that all by yourself, many times over. Justice has been a long time coming for you, but it's finally arriving. Guards, make sure these two are secured. Top-level holding."

Kavana resisted as the guards started to lead them away.

"I have a request," she said.

Val motioned for the guards to pause.

"You're not really in a position to make requests, but, what the hell, let's hear it. Might be good for a larf."

"Go easy on Angela. She's only a child."

"She's almost the same age you were when you started all this. Besides, there really isn't a juvenile court when it comes to trying sedition and conspiracy."

"I know. But I still thought I'd ask. Do whatever you want with Clerak and me, you've earned that, but I'm begging you to show mercy to Angela."

"She'll be tried fairly, is all I can promise. As will the two of you."

Val stood back and allowed the troopers to take the two women away.

Val next made her way to the communication room.

"Hey," she said into the transcriber.

Catherine's visage appeared in the room before her.

"Hello. How goes it?"

"The situation on Kaia's actually been handled," said Val. "You all can come back whenever you like."

"Actually, the kids are having a great time. We thought we'd stay here a bit longer, if it's all the same to you."

"That's fine. Give them my love."

There was barking in the background of Catherine's transmission.

"Yes, John, that includes you, too." Val smiled before terminating the transmission.

It heartened Val to find Neva and Jenneca in the latter girl's bedroom, sat upon the bed and giggling their heads off. She was almost loathe to interrupt their bonding time.

"Good, you're both here," Val said as she finally decided to enter the room.

"We are?" Jenneca asked. "I mean, I know we're here, but I didn't realize here was a thing."

"Well, I have something I want to discuss with you," Val said.

"What is it?" Jenneca asked.

"It's sort of a family thing."

"Oh. I can leave," Neva offered.

"No, you're part of this family," Val said.

"Okay."

"Bontu is thinking of quitting," Val announced.

"He's what?" Jenneca asked. "Why?"

"He's tired of getting beaten up, basically. And he wants to spend more time with his own kids. It's actually kind of unusual for a Guardian to have a family of their own."

"You're an unusual monarch though, aren't you?" Jenneca

asked.

"That is definitely true. But, with him retiring, I'm going to need a new guardian. Maybe not retiring fully just yet, but pulling back from his duties."

"Okay," Jenneca said.

"You interested?"

"Wait, me?" Jenneca asked. "How would that work?"

"You've grown up in the palace. You know what a Guardian's duties are. Bontu's still around, for now. You'd be sort of like his apprentice."

"Yeah, but, isn't a guardian supposed to be able to take up the Crown if they need to?" Jenneca asked.

"That used to be the case, sure. With how it is now, I don't know if anyone should be trying to take up the Crown. Besides, your father wasn't of the blood, and he served as my guardian for almost a year."

"I thought that was just because you were in a rebuilding phase," Jenneca said.

"If things had worked out differently, I'd have been happy to have him here until one of us died. The old rules don't apply anymore, kiddo." Val flashed a quick smile. "And anyway, it was never actually a law that the guardian had to be of the blood. When I was named guardian for your Uncle Joe, no one batted an eye, even if they didn't know I was secretly his sister."

"Mom, if you... if you really want me to, then yes, I'll be your guardian."

"There's no one I'd trust more. You've had years of Trainer's instruction, and if there's any areas where he thinks you're still deficient, believe me, he will work you twice as hard to make those up. This is going to be hard work."

"I'm not afraid of hard work," Jenneca said.

"Yeah, I know. You were ready to start your training with the Crown, before all of this happened. Donnie, that was one more thing he just didn't ever get."

"We don't have to talk about him."

"I know. But at some point, we will. I don't know if you'll

ever... after what he did, if you'll ever miss him, but you'll think about him. And it'll hurt. And hopefully, over time, it'll hurt less."

"Are you going to miss him?" Jenneca asked.

"Jenn, he's my son. No matter what happened, there was a connection there. But let's, um, let's not worry about that sibling. There's another reason I want you to serve as guardian. I might not be around forever. If I go, I talked it over with Joseph and Sanke, and Neva, we think it best if you inherited the Crown."

"Me?!" Neva balked.

"If the Crown can be trusted after this. We're still figuring that out. But, the people love a good story. A king who grew up on a distant world, and a queen who never knew of her heritage."

"I thought they liked a sense of continuity?" Neva remarked.

"They do. They like both, I guess. And I'm not going anywhere anytime soon. Thanks to Jenneca. By the time you might have to worry about taking up the Crown, the people will know you."

"Oh. Okay."

"But you're not ready. Not yet. Not even close. Jenn, she'll need someone to whip her into shape."

"Isn't that what Trainer's for?" Jenneca asked.

"Yeah, he's around to teach her how to fight, tactics, whatever. But she'll need someone who can be at her side, always. She'll need a proper guardian."

"Okay." Jenneca nodded.

"Besides," said Val, "Trainer's not going to be around forever."

"He can't be that old," Jenneca said. "I know he taught you when you were little, but..."

"And my father."

"Wait, really?" Jenneca asked. "How old is he?"

"No one really knows. That's a secret that's more guarded than anything the royal family's got. He's been an old man for as long as anyone can remember."

The girls started giggling again. It gladdened their mother to join them.

CHAPTER 6

On a sunny morning not too long after, Val stood in a castle corridor, looking at a doorway. Bontu and Jenneca, in crisp, matching, white-trimmed black uniforms, flanked her. Several robed mages focused their attention on the doorway in front of them.

"I've lived almost my entire life in this castle," said Val, "I can't believe I've never noticed this doorway before."

"Well, it was shielded by magic," said Bontu.

"And there was a giant pit bore down through the courtyard into it," Val said.

"The magic was very strong," said Bontu.

"We just filled in the pit and left it at that," said Val.

"The Arna Academy sent over their best to unlock it," said Jenneca. "Hopefully we should be good soon."

Under the hands of the trio of mages, the doorway began to vibrate. Sparks flew from its edges.

"Is it supposed to do that?" Val asked.

"No," said one of the mages, "but these are very ancient and powerful magics at work. It was never going to be clean."

"Super." Val looked at her cousin and daughter. "Do we want to take a step back?"

Without another word, the three of them stepped backwards.

The sparking along the door's edges turned into burning. Soon the whole thing was engulfed in an unnatural flame. In a final burst, the doorway cleared.

"Are we good?" Val asked.

"I believe so, my queen."

Val headed into the entry. Jenneca and Bontu followed.

It took some time for the group to make it all the way down the winding stairway towards the buried chamber. Eternally burning torches lit the way.

Val was the first to enter the darkened cavern. She flicked on a lantern and looked around. The shadows of five people could still be seen burned into the walls.

"Huh. So this is where it started."

"I thought it started on Earth," said Bontu.

"Well, yeah, okay, but this is where Angelo's whole thing got kicked into gear."

"Is there something I'm not seeing?" Jenneca asked. "It's just a big old room."

"Very old and big," Bontu agreed.

"It might be more about what the room represents," said Val.

"What does the room represent?" Jenneca asked.

"You know, a plot to overthrow the monarchy," said Val. "Twice. I wonder if the old vizier actually knew what he was doing when he began."

"We could ask him, but Kavana slit his throat," said Jenneca.

"Even if she hadn't, there's a good chance he'd be dead by now anyway," Val said. "He didn't really take great care of himself and indulged in decadence a bit too freely."

"As you're the only one here who ever met the man, we'll have to take your word for it," Bontu said.

Val inhaled deeply.

"You smell that?" she asked.

Jenneca sniffed the air.

"It smells like... sunshine? But in a bad way."

"And what does sunshine smell like?" Bontu asked.

"It smells like it smells," said Jenneca. "It's its own thing."

She turned to her mother. "What are you even going to do with it?"

"I don't know," Val said. "Maybe put in a pool down here?"

"We have pools," said Jenneca.

"What about a wine cellar?" Bontu asked.

"We have a bunch of those, too," said Jenneca.

"I was joking," said Val.

"I also was joking," said Bontu.

"I just didn't like the idea of leaving it how it was," said Val.

They heard the rapid patter of footfalls on stone approaching.

Neva frantically entered the chamber, holding her gown up enough to allow her to run.

"I'm here! I made it, I'm here!"

"Welcome to our finest pit," said Val.

"Yeah, it was weird, I must've walked past this spot like five times today, and then suddenly I found it, but you guys were already gone," said Neva.

"It's okay," Val assured her.

Neva tugged at her dress.

"And I'm not used to making it up and down stairs in a gown."

"I know how that goes," Val said. "But you're here now. That's what matters."

"I am here now," Neva said. "That is factually accurate. What were we talking about?"

"Trying to figure out what to do with this pit," said Val.

"Oh."

"What did it used to be?" Bontu asked.

"We think it was a temple," said Val. "Before the castle was even built. It's definitely out of the way now. We probably don't want to turn it into anything really necessary. Nobody's going to want to go up and down those stairs to get to whatever it becomes."

"We could install an elevator," Jenneca suggested.

Val shrugged.

"Still."

"Is that something we need to decide today?" Neva asked.

Val, Bontu, and Jenneca looked at one another.

"I guess not," Val said. "We were just spit-balling, really."

"You did kind of seem like you wanted an idea," said Jenneca.

"Wanting an idea and requiring one aren't exactly the same thing," said Val. "We can hold off on any big decisions about this place for now. We've been making enough big moves the last few days as it is."

"That is definitely true," said Bontu.

"Cool. So does that mean we don't have to hang around this pit?" Jenneca asked.

"No, we don't."

They started for the exit.

"Aw," Neva groaned. "I just got here."

"Yeah," said Val, "that's also true."

CHAPTER 7

Val sat alone on the royal seal on stone floor. The throne room had been cleared. No attendants, no guardians, no family or friends.

Just her.

Her and her memories.

They came flooding back to her as she concentrated on the Crown of the Fifteen Point Star sat in her lap. She couldn't help it. It was automatic, like it had been after she wore the Crown in battle.

Her thoughts extended back; back to her childhood in the castle, her training in the military, her missions as a special operative, meeting her brother on Earth, and all the battles since.

Her fingertips found their way beneath the lowest curves of the Crown and gently hoisted it up. It was heavier than before.

Energy flowed from its metal into her body. The glowing started in her fingers and worked its way up her arms. She remained focused, controlled.

She methodically turned it around in her hands and moved it towards her forehead.

"Okay. Let's see what happens next."

Made in the USA
Middletown, DE
24 November 2022

15619371R00136